The Tiger's Whisker

HAROLD COURLANDER

The Tiger's Whisker

AND

OTHER TALES AND LEGENDS FROM

ASIA AND THE PACIFIC

ILLUSTRATED BY ENRICO ARNO

HARCOURT, BRACE & WORLD, INC., NEW YORK

© 1959 BY HAROLD COURLANDER

c.5.61

LIBRARY OF CONGRESS CATALOG CARD NUMBER: 59-10172

PRINTED IN THE UNITED STATES OF AMERICA

For Erika, Michael, and Susan

Contents

The Tiger's Whisker

The Scholar of Kosei

A KOREAN TALE

In the village of Kosei lived a great scholar by the name of Pak. He lived his life in deep thought and contemplation, and in studying insects, birds, and flowers. No man in Kosei was more versed in ancient history than Pak, or in the great literature of the land. So deeply immersed was Pak in profound things of this kind that he sometimes behaved a little strangely. He would forget to get up in the morning or forget to go to sleep at night; and once while considering the history of the Korean kings, he sat sipping on an empty teacup for hours.

It happened one time that Pak decided to go to Pyongyang to talk with some other scholars who lived there. His wife and daughter prepared his clothes for him, and he took his staff and began his journey.

When he had been walking for many hours, he came to a spring. He took off his hat and placed it on top of a bush; then he got down on his knees and drank from the spring, all the while thinking of important questions he was going to place before the scholars of Pyongyang. When he arose and started to continue on his way, he saw the bush with a hat on top of it. A wide smile came to his face.

"Some forgetful man has placed his hat there and forgotten to take it away," Pak said to himself. "How ridiculous it looks sitting on top of the bush!"

And shaking his head in amusement, he started off again, never noticing that his own head was bare.

When night came, he found a shelter in a cave near the road. He made himself some tea and sat a long time contemplating on the nature of the universe. Before going to sleep, he cautioned himself:

"The road is long, and the country is strange. I must be careful not to take the wrong path or my journey will be endless. How shall I know, when the sun rises, which way to go?"

He thought about this problem for some time, and at last he solved it. He went out of the cave and laid his staff on the ground, pointing it in the direction of Pyongyang.

"Now there will be no question when I arise as to which way I will travel," Pak said. He returned to the cave and went to sleep.

When the first rays of the sun came in the morning, another traveler came along the road and saw Pak's staff on the ground. He picked it up and examined it. Then he saw Pak sleeping in the cave, so he put the staff back on the ground and walked on. But when he put the staff down, he pointed it in the opposite direction, not at Pyongyang but at the village of Kosei.

Pak soon awoke. He made himself some tea, and when he was ready to travel again, he went out and picked up his staff, carefully noting the direction in which it was pointing.

After several hours he came to a bush with a hat sitting on top. Pak began to laugh.

"What strange things are to be seen on the way to Pyongyang!" he said aloud. "In two days, two bushes wearing hats!"

And after a while Pak saw a village on the hillside.

"Pyongyang!" he said. "I have arrived sooner than I thought possible!"

Just then a man from Kosei passed, and he greeted Pak like a neighbor. Pak returned the greeting, saying to himself: "Oh, but the people of Pyongyang are friendly, not stiff and formal as I imagined."

He examined the rice fields as he walked, thinking: "Why, these gardens don't look a bit different than the gardens at home! I imagined everything would be bigger around Pyongyang."

On the very edge of the village he stopped to look at one garden in particular. "That garden looks just like my own," he said. "How wonderful that things can be so similar even though they are so far apart!"

He entered the village and was struck by its similarity to the place from which he had come. "Pyongyang, why it is no bigger than Kosei! After all the things I have heard about it, it turns out to be just like home. Even the people look the same."

But now Pak began to notice that the people were all staring at him, even the women who should have been much more discreet and proper with a stranger. "What bad manners the people of Pyongyang have!" he thought. "They stare with their eyes and make strangers uncomfortable."

So troubled was Pak with this staring that he opened his fan and held it in front of his face. He began to feel anger rising inside him. "Ah, the women of Pyongyang! They should be taught manners! The big city is indeed a bad place!"

Peeking around his fan, Pak saw with horror that a beautiful young lady was approaching him. He stopped in his tracks, unable to believe his eyes. He heard her speak to him. He stood as though frozen to the ground. At first he didn't comprehend the words. Then he thought: "Ah, the dialect here is quite like that in Kosei." He turned his eyes on the beautiful young lady who was speaking to him. "She looks familiar," he thought. "Where could I ever have met her before?" And while his mind was busy with this problem, it came to him. "She resembles my own daughter!" he said aloud. "What a remarkable thing!"

Then, at last, he really began to hear what the young lady was saying.

"Father, how does it happen that you are back so soon from Pyongyang? And where is your hat?"

"Back? My hat?" Pak said, wondering how his daughter had got to Pyongyang ahead of him.

Then he saw a woman who looked very much like his wife standing in a doorway of a house that looked very much like his own. "Strange, strange!" Pak muttered. "The world is so small and familiar!"

"Don't stand this way in front of your own house," the woman said. "Come in and rest yourself after your long journey."

It was only then that Pak realized that his journey had ended. He entered his house and rested, thinking deeply. Finally he sighed and said:

"The great scholars of Pyongyang are not what they are supposed to be. They had no answers for anything. I can't remember a single thing they said."

The Tiger's Whisker

A KOREAN TALE

A young woman by the name of Yun Ok came one day to the house of a mountain hermit to seek his help. The hermit was a sage of great renown and a maker of charms and magic potions.

When Yun Ok entered his house, the hermit said, without raising his eyes from the fireplace into which he was looking: "Why are you here?"

Yun Ok said: "Oh, Famous Sage, I am in distress! Make me a potion!"

"Yes, yes, make a potion! Everyone needs potions! Can we cure a sick world with a potion?"

"Master," Yun Ok replied, "if you do not help me, I am truly lost!"

"Well, what is your story?" the hermit said, resigned at last to listen.

"It is my husband," Yun Ok said. "He is very dear to me. For the past three years he has been away fighting in the wars. Now that he has returned, he hardly speaks to me, or to anyone else. If I speak, he doesn't seem to hear. When he talks at all, it is roughly. If I serve him food not to his liking, he pushes it aside and angrily leaves the room. Sometimes when he should be working in the rice field, I see him sitting idly on top of the hill, looking toward the sea."

"Yes, so it is sometimes when young men come back from the wars," the hermit said. "Go on."

"There is no more to tell, Learned One. I want a potion to give my husband so that he will be loving and gentle, as he used to be."

"Ha, so simple, is it?" the hermit said. "A potion! Very well; come back in three days and I will tell you what we shall need for such a potion."

Three days later Yun Ok returned to the home of the mountain sage. "I have looked into it," he told her. "Your potion can be made. But the most essential ingredient is the whisker of a living tiger. Bring me this whisker and I will give you what you need."

"The whisker of a living tiger!" Yun Ok said. "How could I possibly get it?"

"If the potion is important enough, you will succeed," the hermit said. He turned his head away, not wishing to talk any more.

Yun Ok went home. She thought a great deal about how she would get the tiger's whisker. Then one night when her husband was asleep, she crept from her house with a bowl of rice and meat sauce in her hand. She went to the place on the mountainside where the tiger was known to live. Standing far off from the tiger's cave, she held out the bowl of food, calling the tiger to come and eat. The tiger did not come.

The next night Yun Ok went again, this time a little bit closer. Again she offered a bowl of food. Every night Yun Ok went to the mountain, each time a few steps nearer the tiger's cave than the night before. Little by little the tiger became accustomed to seeing her there.

One night Yun Ok approached to within a stone's throw of the tiger's cave. This time the tiger came a few steps toward her and stopped. The two of them stood looking at one another in the moonlight. It happened again the following night, and this time they were so close that Yun Ok could talk to the tiger in a soft, soothing voice. The next night, after looking carefully into Yun Ok's eyes, the tiger ate the food that she held out for him. After that when Yun Ok came in the night, she found the tiger waiting for her on the trail. When the tiger had eaten, Yun Ok could gently rub his head with her hand. Nearly six months had passed since the night of her first visit. At last one night, after caressing the animal's head, Yun Ok said:

"Oh, Tiger, generous animal, I must have one of your whiskers. Do not be angry with me!"

And she snipped off one of the whiskers.

The tiger did not become angry, as she had feared he might. Yun Ok went down the trail, not walking but running, with the whisker clutched tightly in her hand.

The next morning she was at the mountain hermit's house just as the sun was rising from the sea. "Oh, Famous One!" she cried, "I have it! I have the tiger's whisker! Now you can make me the potion you promised so that my husband will be loving and gentle again!"

The hermit took the whisker and examined it. Satisfied that it had really come from a tiger, he leaned forward and dropped it into the fire that burned in his fireplace.

"Oh, sir!" the young woman called in anguish. "What have you done with it!"

"Tell me how you obtained it," the hermit said.

"Why, I went to the mountain each night with a little bowl of food. At first I stood afar, and I came a little closer each time, gaining the tiger's confidence. I spoke gently and soothingly to him, to make him understand I wished him only good. I was patient. Each night I brought him food, knowing that he would not eat. But I did not give up. I came again and again. I never spoke harshly. I never reproached him. And at last one night he took a few steps toward me. A time came when he would meet me on the trail and eat out of the bowl that I held in my hands.

I rubbed his head, and he made happy sounds in his throat. Only after that did I take the whisker."

"Yes, yes," the hermit said, "you tamed the tiger and won his confidence and love."

"But you have thrown the whisker in the fire!" Yun Ok cried. "It is all for nothing!"

"No, I do not think it is all for nothing," the hermit said. "The whisker is no longer needed. Yun Ok, let me ask you, is a man more vicious than a tiger? Is he less responsive to kindness and understanding? If you can win the love and confidence of a wild and bloodthirsty animal by gentleness and patience, surely you can do the same with your husband?"

Hearing this, Yun Ok stood speechless for a moment. Then she went down the trail, turning over in her mind the truth she had learned in the house of the mountain hermit.

The Tiger's Minister of State

A SHAN TALE FROM BURMA

Word went through the forest one day that Kyar the tiger, king of animals, needed a chief minister of state. So, from the places where they lived, Wet-wun the boar, Myauk the monkey, and Yon the rabbit set out for the tiger's house. Coming from different directions, they arrived on the same day. They gathered before Kyar's gate and waited until the king saw fit to let them in.

The tiger king at last came out of his house, looking lean and hungry.

"Who are these people standing before my gate?" he asked his servants.

"They are Wet-wun the boar, Myauk the monkey, and Yon the rabbit," his servants replied. "They are applying for the job of minister of state."

"Let them in," Kyar the tiger said.

The servants opened the gate, and the three animals entered and sat on the ground before the king.

"It is true, as you have heard, that I need a new minister," the tiger said. "However, the one I select for this position must have the gift of being able to say the right thing at the right time. My last minister didn't have the ability."

"I have the ability," Wet-wun the boar said.

"No, I have the ability," Myauk the monkey said.

"On the contrary, it is I who have the ability," Yon the rabbit said.

"Well, since you can't agree, I'll have to ask you to pass

an examination," Kyar the tiger said. "He who speaks most wisely will be my minister. Boar, come forward."

The boar came forward.

The tiger opened his mouth and asked him: "Is my breath sweet or not?"

The boar smelled the king's breath. It was foul. But he was eager to please Kyar, so he said: "Oh Great King, never have I smelled such a sweet breath! It is like fruit blossoms in full bloom!"

"Ah, just as I thought," the tiger said. "You are a flatterer. A flatterer has no regard for the truth, but only for his own welfare. Such a man would be a danger to me and my kingdom." And he pounced on the boar and ate him.

Then Kyar called on the monkey to come forward.

"Is my breath sweet or not?" he asked, opening his mouth wide.

The monkey was more cautious. He smelled the tiger's breath. "Hm!" he said.

"Well?" Kyar asked.

"Just a moment," the monkey said, and he sniffed again.

"Answer the question," the tiger ordered.

"Oh Great One," the monkey said at last, "you will see that I am no flatterer. You can always rely on me for the truth. For your breath indeed smells very bad."

"Smells bad, did you say?" the tiger asked, his eyes opening very wide.

"Yes, quite offensive. Please don't ask me to sniff again."

"So! It is just as I suspected," the tiger king said. "You are the kind of person who speaks directly, without any regard for anyone's feelings. It is this kind of minister that creates arguments and bad feelings everywhere. Such a man is a menace to the community."

And Kyar the tiger pounced on Myauk the monkey and

ate him. As he finished eating, he wiped his mouth and turned to Yon the rabbit.

"Now it is your turn," he said. "Is my breath foul, as the monkey said, or sweet, as the boar said?"

He opened his mouth, and the rabbit came forward and sniffed. As he sniffed, his nose twitched. He sniffed and twitched in front of the tiger's mouth, but gave no answer.

"Well, what is it? Foul or sweet?" the tiger demanded.

The rabbit came a little closer, his nose twitching violently. At last he said: "Oh King, how unfortunate I am!"

"What is the trouble?" Kyar asked.

"I have a terrible cold," the rabbit replied. "I can't smell a thing one way or the other."

The tiger smiled.

"You are the man to be my minister!" he said. "For an ordinary person a sense of smell is important. But one who deals in affairs of state is better off without one."

And he appointed Yon, the rabbit, to be his minister of state. The rabbit is still the tiger's minister of state. And day in, day out, he twitches his nose to show the king that he still has a cold and can't smell a thing one way or the other.

The Trial of the Stone

A SHAN TALE FROM BURMA

A young boy named Than was traveling on the road from his village to his grandfather's village. He walked all day, and when night came, he found a place by the side of the road, on the outskirts of a small town, where he could sleep. But in his pocket he carried a few small coins, all the money he owned, and he worried that while he slept someone would come and take it from him. So he searched around and found a large stone. He moved the stone a little and placed his money under it. Then, when he was sure that it was safe until morning, he lay down and slept.

But an unscrupulous man of the town had seen Than hide the money, and when the boy was sound asleep, the man came and took it and went away.

Than slept until sunrise. He went to a stream and washed. Then he went to the stone to get his money, thinking he would buy a small breakfast in the town. He reached under the stone with his hand, but he felt nothing but the dry earth. He turned the stone over and saw there was nothing there. Than stood by the roadside and cried.

People of the town who happened to pass by stopped and tried to comfort him. Soon there was a crowd standing around. After a while the town chief came and demanded to know what was going on.

"Last night I slept by the side of the road," the boy said. "I hid my money under a stone. When morning came, I looked under the stone but the money was gone."

The judge looked serious. He frowned. People waited to see what he would do about this strange affair.

"Where is this stone?" he asked at last.

"Here is the stone," the boy said, and he led the town chief and the townspeople to the place he had hidden the money.

"Is this the stone?" the chief asked.

"This is the stone," the boy answered.

"Arrest it!" the chief said sternly. "It will stand trial for robbery!"

The people stood in amazement, not believing what they had heard.

"Why do you stand there?" the chief said. "Is not this the stone that is accused of stealing the boy's money?"

So the townsmen picked up the stone that Than had pointed out and carried it to the place where the town trials were held. The chief sat down. The clerk who kept the records was ready with his paper and pen. The townspeople crowded all around. The officers of the court sat in their usual positions. The chief ordered the suspect brought forward to answer the charge of robbery on the highway. Two men carried the stone through the crowd and put it down in front of the chief, who glared at it ferociously.

The townspeople looked at one another and tried not to laugh, or even smile, while the chief asked the stone questions.

"Do you admit robbing the boy of his money?" the chief asked.

The stone said nothing, of course, and the chief said to the clerk: "Put down on the record that the suspect refused to answer." Then he asked the stone: "What were you doing at the edge of the road? What village are you from?"

Still the stone was silent. The people in the crowd covered their faces with their hands to keep from laughing. As for the chief, he looked very serious about the matter, and he stared at the stone grimly.

"What is your name? How old are you?" he asked.

Now there was snickering through the crowd of spectators. Some people snorted uncontrollably through their noses. The chief took his eyes off the suspected thief long enough to look around and say:

"There must be no laughing here! This is a court of law! You are warned!"

Then he looked back at the stone accusingly. "As for you, you will not get off easily just by keeping quiet! Speak up! Where were you when the boy went to sleep? And what did you do with the money you took?"

As the stone continued to be silent the chief of the town raised his voice and shouted: "Ha! You mock the law? You are sentenced to thirty lashes, after which your head will be cut off!"

When the townspeople heard this, they couldn't restrain themselves any longer. A man snorted, a woman squealed, and instantly everyone was choking with laughter. The sound of the laughing rose to a roar. Once started they couldn't stop.

Through it all the judge remained calm, waiting for the noise to come to an end. At last the crowd fell silent, worn out with laughing. The chief turned to the clerk and said:

"Enter into your records that upon hearing the judgment against the thieving stone, the spectators in the court raised a huge commotion, indicating ridicule of the magistrate. I therefore fine each spectator one penny for contempt." Turning back to the surprised crowd, the chief ordered: "Come forward one at a time and leave your penalty with the clerk."

Not even smiling now, the spectators formed a line, and one at a time they paid their fines. Then the judge gathered the coins in his hand and presented them to the boy Than,

saying: "For the injury you suffered, our town offers you this compensation."

And the chief then sent Than on his way.

As for the stone, the people carried it to the edge of the town and gave it thirty lashes. But as for beheading it, they were perplexed how to begin. Instead, they gave it a few extra lashes and left it by the roadside to ponder the fate of thieves.

The Hidden Treasure of Khin

A BURMESE TALE

A young man named Khin one day grew dissatisfied with his life in the village, and when he came home from the rice fields with his father, he said:

"What kind of life is this? We work from sunup to nightfall, and when it is over, we eat a little rice, and that is all there is to living. I think I will go to the city and become rich."

Khin's father was sad. He said: "I had hoped to share my house and fields with you for many years. Yet if you are sure this way of life is not for you, go on your way." He gave Khin a little silver money that he had hidden under the ground, and as his parting words the father said:

"Though we may not see each other again, there are few words of guidance I can give you. The city is big, and trees don't bear golden fruit. Just as here in these fields, in the city one must work if he is to live. These things you will have to learn for yourself. If there is one thing I can say to guide you, it is this: Only hidden treasure is worthwhile."

Khin went away. He felt free at last of the village and its boredom. He pondered what his father had said, but he could make no sense out of it. "What kind of words are these? Hidden treasure is of no use to anyone. Treasure is good only when it is discovered."

When he arrived in the big city of Mandalay, he saw great wealth all around him, and he said: "Ah, this is good! Here I will work and become rich!"

But the months went by and Khin did not become rich. The years went by and he became poorer. Life wasn't at all good to him. He worked as a servant for a rich man, but his wages were small and he couldn't save a thing. He heard tales of people who had found jars of gold in the ground, but Khin found nothing. As time passed, he thought more and more of the old life in the village.

One day a stranger came to the place where he lived in the servants' quarters of the rich man's house, saying: "I am looking for Khin, the son of Nu."

"I am Khin, the son of Nu," Khin said.

"I am from the village of Mawlu, and I have a message for you. Your old father has died. But before he died, he asked me to find you and to say that he has left two full bags of treasure for you in case you should ever come home."

Khin wept that his father had died and that he had remembered Khin at the moment of death. He thanked the villager, and then he took his few clothes and his knife and began the long journey home.

As he walked along the road, he kept thinking of the treasure his father had left behind. "Who would have guessed it? We lived so poorly," Khin said to himself.

When he arrived in his village, he went to his old home, but it was empty. He went then to his uncle's house. His uncle greeted him and fed him, and they talked.

At last his uncle said: "As you heard, your father left two bags of treasure for you. But they are yours only on one condition, that you bury them in the ground."

Khin thought in amazement: "What silliness is this? I am poor and wretched, and my father has left me treasure, and now I must put it in the ground!" He remembered then his father's last words to him when he was leaving the village: "Only hidden treasure is worthwhile."

Khin said to his uncle: "I cannot understand. But if my father made this condition, this is the way it must be."

The uncle then uncovered two large bags in the corner of the room. Khin was amazed at their size. He could not imagine such wealth. He went to the first bag and opened it. He was bewildered, for it was full of rice. He opened the second bag. It, too, was full of rice. He was silent for a while, and then he asked his uncle: "Is this a joke?"

His uncle replied: "No, these are the bags that your father left for you, with instructions that you bury them."

Slowly Khin began to understand. He took the bags to his father's house and slept there. In the morning he carried them out to the fields and began to bury the rice in the ground, one grain at a time. The weeks went by and the rice sprouted, and when it was grown, he harvested it and had many times as much rice as he had started with. The next year he buried his treasure in the same way, until eventually he became a prosperous farmer in the village of Mawlu.

The King Who Ate Chaff

A BURMESE TALE

Once a king went for a walk through the outskirts of his city. As he didn't want to be recognized by his subjects, he disguised himself as a common merchant and took only a single servant with him. He looked on with interest at all the things that ordinary people were doing, and at last he turned back toward home. At that moment he saw an old woman winnowing rice. The chaff that the woman threw away smelled very sweet to the king, and suddenly he had an overpowering desire to eat some of it. He walked on a few steps, and then ordered his servant to go back and bring him some chaff to eat.

The servant was shocked. He protested that it was a disgraceful thing for a great king to eat chaff, which was food fit only for cows and pigs. But the king told him not to give advice, and spoke angrily. So the servant brought him the chaff, and the king ate it eagerly, as though he had never tasted anything so good. When he was through, he spoke sternly to his servant, saying: "If you say the slightest word to anyone about this affair, you will lose your head."

After they had returned to the king's house, the servant was overcome with an irresistible urge to tell someone what he had seen. He couldn't sleep for thinking about it. He lost his appetite. He did everything he could think of to help him forget. Nothing helped. "If I could even whisper it to someone I would feel better," he thought. But he didn't dare to say a word.

Two or three days passed. The servant became ill and haggard from lack of sleep, and worst of all the itch to tell his secret still tortured him. At last, unable to bear it any longer, he rushed out of the house to a grove of trees where he could whisper the words without anyone hearing him. But there was a woodcutter nearby, so he got in a boat and rowed himself out to the middle of the river. He saw fishermen there, so he fled back to the shore and went to the cemetery, but once there he thought the gravediggers might overhear him. At last he went out to the forest, and putting his head into the hollow of a big tree, he whispered fervently: "The great king eats chaff! The great king eats chaff! The great king eats chaff!" After that he felt better and went home.

Many months later, the great palace drum, which announced the hours, cracked and broke, and the royal drum makers went into the forest and cut down a tree for a new drum. It happened that the tree they chose was the very one into which the servant had whispered his terrible secret.

In a few weeks the new drum was ready. It was a beautiful drum. Everyone looked at it and admired it. It was installed with pomp and ceremony on its stone platform. The king and his court and visitors from the city and the countryside stood and watched.

At the height of the ceremony the drum was beaten for the first time. The people were amazed, because the drum did not say "boom, boom" as the old drum had. Instead, it said: "The great king eats chaff! The great king eats chaff! The great king eats chaff!"

The Musician of Tagaung

A BURMESE TALE

In the town of Tagaung, it is said, there was once a man
with an only son. The boy's name was Maung Pon. A time
came when the father decided the boy must have a profes-
sion.

"In the whole history of my family there has never
been a musician," the man said to himself. "What kind of
family can we be? My son shall be a great harp player and
bring credit to us all."

He went out and bought for Maung Pon a beautiful
gilded harp with silk strings, and engaged one of the best
musicians of Tagaung to teach him how to play it.

The boy took his harp each day and went to the teacher's
house. But Maung Pon was not good at learning to play the
harp. The teacher would explain, and Maung Pon tried
earnestly, but he was clumsy and heavy-handed and he
simply broke the strings as he tried to play.

Each week the father bought more strings, stronger
strings, and the harp was restrung. The teacher went on
explaining, but Maung Pon couldn't get it in his head that
the harp was a delicate instrument, and his awkward fingers
went on breaking strings.

The teacher gave up hope that the boy would ever learn
anything, but the father paid more and more for the lessons,
so the patient man kept trying.

Years passed, and finally the old teacher died. Maung
Pon's father found a new teacher, and still the young man

didn't learn to play the harp. One day the father died, but his wife kept buying strings for Maung Pon. Maung Pon fell in love and married. He had seven children. They grew up, married, and had their own children. Maung Pon was now an old man, and he took harp lessons from teachers who were much younger than he. Sometimes he would decide he couldn't play because his instrument was no good, and then he would go out and buy another harp.

Finally, lying in bed and resting his head against his harp in weariness, Maung Pon died. Gradually the people in Tagaung forgot him. His old harps were stored in the houses of his children and his grandchildren.

After many years had passed, one of Maung Pon's descendants found an old dusty harp in the corner of his house and asked: "Wherever did we get this old thing?"

Someone replied: "Why, I remember vaguely. They say we had an ancestor by the name of . . . let me see . . . Maung Pon or something. He played the harp. They say he was a great harp player."

They questioned some of their relatives, who looked in their own storage places, and many of them found old harps. They all began to talk about Maung Pon, the great harp player who was their ancestor, and told stories about his tender playing. At first there were some arguments as to whether Maung Pon did this or that, but a day came at last when their stories were all the same and they spoke of him with reverence.

Thus it was that after ninety-seven years Maung Pon fulfilled his father's hopes.

The Rice Puller of Chaohwa

A CHINESE TALE

Near the village of Chaohwa, it is said, there lived a farmer by the name of Liu. He was not very different from the other farmers of Chaohwa, except that he was known as an impatient man. Some of his neighbors referred to him as Liu Always-in-a-hurry. When there was work to be done, he was always urging his wife and sons to go faster. If his wife had to go to the village for something or other, Liu practically pushed her out the door to get her started, and when she returned, he demanded to know what had kept her so long. When he was on the road himself, he was always stepping on the heels of anyone in front of him. He had an uncontrollable desire to be first in everything he did.

One day when Liu was in Chaohwa, he heard a group of farmers talking about their rice fields.

"My rice is sprouting very well," one of them said. "It is nearly two inches high."

Another farmer said, "Yes, my rice is doing well also. It is perhaps a little more than two inches high. In fact, nearly three."

"It is a good year for me, too," a third man said. "In some parts of my field the rice is nearly four inches tall already."

As Liu listened, he became very impatient with his own rice, which certainly wasn't four inches tall, or even three. Probably it wasn't even two.

He hurried back to his fields, stepping on quite a few heels as he went. He even took a short cut, trampling through the mud of a neighbor's rice field. When he saw the rice sprouts in his own fields, his heart fell. They were so short that he could hardly believe what he saw. Not one of them was more than two inches tall.

He hurried home thoughtfully and pondered rapidly over his problem. When his wife and sons spoke to him, he hardly heard them. All night long he rolled and tossed sleeplessly. But just before dawn, he sat upright suddenly, shouting: "I will help them!"

He went to his fields, reached down, and took hold of one of the sprouts with his fingers. Then he pulled ever so gently. The sprout came up a little. "Aha, that's better!" Liu said. Then he pulled the next stalk up a little, then the next. He went through the field this way and that, pulling on the stalks as fast as he could. All day he did this, and in the evening he came home weary and worn.

The next day he rushed again to his fields and began again at the beginning. When he returned home at night-fall, he told his family: "Oh, I am tired! I worked so hard today! But the rice is much taller now, and I am happy!"

Liu's family was surprised at the news, for rice grows ever so slowly. So in the morning they went out together to see the results of Liu's hard work.

What they found was sad to see, for the rice stalks lay withered and dead in the morning sun.

"Alas, is this gratitude?" Liu cried out to the ruined field. "Is this my reward for giving you a helping hand?"

As for the people of Chaohwa, when the news got around, they had to laugh at the outcome of Liu's impatience. And although Liu himself was forgotten as new generations were born and died in Chaohwa, people still say to someone who is overly eager: "Don't be a rice puller."

The Spear and Shield of Huan-Tan

A CHINESE TALE

Once in the old days there was a weapons maker named Huan-Tan, a man who never overlooked any kind of argument that would help to sell his spears and shields. For Huan-Tan, no remark was too extravagant when he praised the qualities of the weapons he made.

One day Huan-Tan was standing in his shop, calling to the crowd of people that surged back and forth in the street. He waved one of his spears in the air and cried out:

"If there are soldiers among you, here is the spear you are looking for! The hardest steel that was ever forged! The sharpest edge that ever was honed! A shaft that is light as the wind! This spear has a will of its own! It cannot be blunted; its edge can never be dulled! And, soldiers, listen to this: The spear I hold in my hand will go through any armor that was ever made! It will go through the toughest metal that is known to man!"

Some of the passers-by stopped to listen as Huan-Tan paid this tribute to his spear. One of them said: "It isn't a spear that I'm looking for, but a shield."

Hearing this, Huan-Tan put down the spear and took up one of his new shields.

"My friend," he said, "this is the shield you are looking for! The hardest steel that is known to man! Look at that polished surface! There is no blade in the world that can dent it or scratch it! Where is the spear that can penetrate

this shield? Nowhere, my friend, because it has never been made!"

The man to whom Huan-Tan was directing this speech was thoughtful.

"Yes, yes," he said, "a wonderful thing. Here you have a shield that can't be penetrated by any spear in existence. And there beside you is a spear that can penetrate anything. Now, how about giving us a demonstration? Why don't you try your wonderful spear against your wonderful shield and let us see what happens?"

The enthusiastic weapons maker looked at the shield in his hand, then at the spear leaning against the wall. His eyes went from one to the other, back and forth, and he was unable to utter a word.

Suddenly he cupped his hand to his ear, saying: "Hark!" He appeared to listen intently for a moment. Then he laid down the shield and said: "It is my wife calling again." And Huan-Tan disappeared into the darkness of the back room of his shop.

A great roar of laughter went up outside, and then the spectators drifted away.

The Ambassador from Chi

A CHINESE TALE

In ancient times, people say, there was bad feeling between the Prince of Chu and the Prince of Chi. But the Prince of Chi wanted to have better relations with the State of Chu, and so he sent an ambassador to the capital of that state.

When the Prince of Chu heard that an ambassador was coming, he decided that he would ridicule the man in public to show his contempt for the country from which he came.

When the ambassador arrived, the Prince of Chu ordered that he be admitted to the palace not by the great central gate, but by a small entrance reserved for domestic servants. The guards directed the Ambassador from Chi to the servant's entrance, but the Ambassador did not enter. He asked: "Is this the gate through which citizens and celebrated personages go in?"

"Oh, no," the guards replied, "the people of Chu go through the great central gate."

"I would like to enter here, for your sake," the Ambassador said. "But you see, I have the strictest orders from the prince of my country. He has instructed me to conform to the habits and customs of the state to which I have been sent. Therefore, as I have been sent to a country of dogs, I will go in through the dogs' gate."

And he went then to the main gate of the palace and entered.

When the Prince of Chu heard of the Ambassador's

reply to his intended insult, he decided to leave no stone unturned to put the man in his place.

Soon afterwards the Prince of Chu gave a formal banquet to which all foreign dignitaries present in the capital were invited, including the Ambassador from Chi. While the festivities were going on, two soldiers entered the banquet hall, dragging with them a handcuffed prisoner. And as instructed by the Prince of Chu, they declared: "At last we have caught him!"

All eyes turned toward the prisoner. The Ambassador from Chi turned to the Prince and asked: "What kind of crime has this man committed?"

The Prince of Chu spoke in a voice that was heard by all, even in the farthest corners of the hall.

"Why, this man is an unscrupulous bandit. He has committed dozens of crimes. He has looted many homes, even stealing from the poor. As a matter of fact, this fellow is a countryman of yours. He comes from the State of Chi. Of course, you won't think that very unusual, I am sure, for everyone knows that most of the people of Chi are bandits and thieves."

The Ambassador from Chi listened very thoughtfully, and when it was his turn to speak, there was no need to raise his voice, for everyone in the hall was listening intently for his reply. He said:

"Oh Prince of Chu, it is well known that oranges growing on the south bank of the Hui River are large, sweet, and nourishing. It is also known that when these fine oranges are transplanted to the north bank of the river, they change their character completely; they become small, sour, and bitter, and are of no use to anyone. This sort of thing also happens to people. The people of my country are hardworking, moral, and law-abiding. But when they go to other countries, they frequently take on the character of the people they find there. You see, it is only when a citizen of Chi comes to the State of Chu that he turns sour and becomes a bandit."

The Prince of Chu was deeply embarrassed at the way his carefully planned insult had been turned against him. But he kept smiling and resolved to find a way to ridicule the Ambassador beyond repair. After a while he said casually: "I understand that there are very few people living in your country."

"On the contrary," the Ambassador said, "we are really very crowded with people. In our capital city alone there are more than eight thousand families. Why, during the day when people are out on the streets, they are jammed shoulder to shoulder. If they all raise their arms together, their sleeves blot out the light of the sun and cast a dark shadow on the ground."

Again the Prince of Chu raised his voice so that everyone in the hall might hear.

"If there are really so many people in the State of Chi, why in the world has your prince selected you, of all men, to be Ambassador to Chu? Couldn't he find a better choice among all the citizens of your country?"

Again there was silence in the hall as the Ambassador answered. He said:

"Oh, Prince of Chu, you see it is this way. In my country we have a guiding principle about sending ambassadors abroad. We send a good man to a state with a good ruler. To a state with a bad and vulgar ruler we send a bad and vulgar ambassador. So, as I am the most useless and worthless man in all of Chi, I was sent to the court of the Prince of Chu."

On hearing his third insult turned against him, the Prince of Chu fell silent, and thus ended his plan to ridicule the State of Chi.

The King of the Forest

A CHINESE FABLE

A fox was searching for something to eat in the forest one day when a large tiger jumped upon him in the tall grass. The tiger held the squirming fox with a single paw. He switched his tail back and forth and prepared to eat his victim. Seeing that he could never squirm free, the fox stopped struggling. He swallowed hard, so that his voice wouldn't tremble. Then he said: "How dare you treat the king of the forest this way?"

The tiger's eyes opened wide in amazement, and his tail stopped switching.

"You are *what?*" he asked.

"I am king of the forest," the fox answered. "God recently appointed me to this position."

"I never heard such nonsense," the tiger said. "No one ever told me that the fox had been made king."

"Ah, then you are the only one who doesn't know about it," the fox told him. "All the other creatures of the forest know about it. They run for their lives when I approach."

"Incredible," the tiger answered.

"Do you want the proof?"

"Yes, prove it to me."

"First, let go of me," the fox said.

The tiger removed his paw from the fox, and the fox got to his feet.

"Now," the fox said, "follow me." He trotted off through the forest with the tiger at his heels. They came to

where a herd of deer were drinking at a watering hole. When the deer saw the tiger approaching, they didn't even notice the fox trotting in front, and they fled in wild disorder. When the monkeys saw the tiger coming, they scrambled into the nearest trees. When the tiger and the fox came to where the elephants were grazing, the elephant herd took one look and ran away. Wherever the tiger and the fox walked, the other animals scattered and ran.

At last the fox turned to the tiger patiently, saying: "Do you need more proof than this that all animals of the forest fear me and flee at my approach?"

The tiger answered: "I have seen enough. I wouldn't have believed it if I hadn't seen it with my own eyes. Forgive me, oh king of the forest, for not recognizing you!"

And the tiger and the fox went separate ways, each looking for his dinner.

The Trial at Avichára-pura

A TALE FROM CEYLON

It happened one time in the village of Avichára-pura that a band of thieves broke into the house of a rich man and stole his money and jewelry. The victim reported the robbery, and police officers went out at once in search of the thieves. They found them nearby and brought them into court.

The judge then listened to the complaint of the man whose property had been stolen. Turning to the thieves, he asked them: "Do you have anything to say in your defense?"

"Yes," the thieves replied. "We weren't really to blame for the robbery at all. It was the man who built the house who was responsible. He made the walls badly. They were thin and rotten and broke through at the slightest push. If it hadn't been for the weak walls, we never would have been tempted to break into the house and steal."

The judge frowned and pondered over this reply. "That is reasonable," he said at last, "very reasonable." And he ordered that the mason who had constructed the house should be brought before him. When the mason arrived, he was accused of responsibility for the theft at the rich man's house.

"You see what your bad work has come to," the judge said sadly. "It has ended in crime."

"Oh, but the fault wasn't mine," the mason said. "It was the laborer who mixed the mortar who was responsible.

49

He was careless, and the mortar he gave me to work with was so badly mixed that it wouldn't hold the stones together."

Hearing this, the judge shook his head solemnly and sent for the laborer who had mixed the mortar. When he came and heard of the crime he was charged with, he said: "Oh, but it wasn't my fault. It is true that the mortar wasn't good. But the culprit is the potter who sold me a cracked pot, which wouldn't hold enough water to mix the mortar properly."

The judge frowned at this news, and he sent for the potter. "You see what your bad pot has brought you to," the judge said sternly. "Because of your poor work a crime has been committed. Do you have anything to say for yourself?"

"Indeed I do," the potter said. "A beautiful woman was the cause of it all. You see, just as I was working on that pot, she passed by, and I couldn't take my eyes from her. It was while I was looking at her that the pot developed a flaw."

Now the judge's temper was rising. "Bring the woman in!" he ordered.

The police went out and found the woman and brought her into court.

"So!" the judge said sternly. "At last it has been revealed that you are the one responsible for the robbery! Just when the potter was working on the pot, you went by and distracted him. He made a bad pot, which didn't hold enough water to make decent mortar, so that the walls of the house were weak and tempted these men here to enter and go off with money and jewels. Do you have any defense?"

The woman answered: "I wouldn't have been near the potter's place at all if the goldsmith had sent my earrings as he had promised to do. I had to go after them myself, and I had to pass the potter's house. The guilt belongs to the goldsmith."

Then the judge angrily ordered the goldsmith brought in and accused him of the crime. The goldsmith couldn't think of a single word to say in his own defense. The judge roared at him to speak, but the goldsmith was speechless. At last the judge ordered the man to be hanged.

But the people of the village protested. They said: "After all, we do need a goldsmith in our village. Can't you suspend the sentence?"

"A crime has been committed," the judge said sternly, "and someone must hang for it!"

"Well, you are right," the villagers said. "Justice is justice, and someone must hang. But since the goldsmith can't be spared, let us hang the first stranger who comes through Avichára-pura."

"That is a wise solution," the judge said thoughtfully. And he decreed then and there that the first stranger to arrive in the village should be strung up without any further talk. The case was closed, and the court adjourned.

When word of the trial went from one place to another, people stopped coming to Avichára-pura altogether. And after that, whenever some silly act was carried out in the name of justice, people said: "It's just like the trial at Avichára-pura."

The Prince of the Six Weapons

AN INDIAN TALE

In ancient times there was a Raja in Benares by the name of Brahmadatta. It is said that the Raja had a son, and when the boy was grown, the Raja called upon his priests to foretell what the boy's future would be. The priests studied the stars in the skies and recalled that the heavens had been luminous when the Raja's son was born. They consulted with each other for many days until they were agreed on the omens and signs. At last they came before the Raja and said:

"Great Ruler, the stars testify that your son will be fearless, proud, and good. In days to come he will rule over Benares as you now rule over it, with piety, courage, and wisdom. In future years he will come to be known as the Prince of the Six Weapons."

"How is this?" the Raja asked. "Is it not known that there are but five weapons—the bow, the spear, the shield, the war-ax, and the sword?"

"It is not known to us, the sixth weapon," the priests said.

"No matter; the stars have revealed a good fate for him," the Raja replied. "The nature of the sixth weapon will be known in time."

And he called his son and told him that he was now a young man and that it was time for him to acquire higher learning.

"In the city of Cawnpore lives a great teacher. There you will go and study. When you have learned all that he can teach you, return to Benares to help me rule my kingdom with wisdom and strength."

The Raja's son made preparations and set out for Cawnpore. He found the great teacher about whom his father had spoken, and he lived there and learned. Five years he remained in Cawnpore. He learned of astronomy, of history, and of the sayings of great sages. And at last his teacher said to him:

"Were we to sit together until the mountains melt away in the rains we could not explore all the secrets of nature. Your father waits for your homecoming. I have no more to teach you."

And so the Raja's son said good-by to his teacher and began the long journey home. He wore five weapons now—the bow, the spear, the war-ax, the sword, and the shield.

As he journeyed, he came to a forest, and people cried out to him: "Don't enter here! This is the forest of the Hairy Demon!"

"I fear no demons," he replied, and he went into the forest that lay between him and the city of Benares.

The great trees shut out the sun, so that the young man walked in a half-light that was neither day nor night. And where the trail touched upon the bank of a wild river, he came upon a monstrous creature standing in an attitude of waiting. The Hairy Demon was as high as the tallest forest trees. His face was like that of a great wild boar, but his mouth was that of a hawk, and from its corners there grew two ivory tusks longer than those of the king of all elephants. The Demon's feet were shaped like those of a tiger. His head and his body were covered with coarse blue hair, which covered him completely and hung to the ground.

The Raja's son stopped in wonder as he saw the monster, but he didn't run. He said: "Monster, why do you stand across the trail when I wish to pass?"

"The trail ends here," the Hairy Demon answered. "This

is my feeding place, and few travelers come this way any more."

"I do not fear you," the Raja's son said. "I am the Prince of the Six Weapons. Stand aside or I will force you."

"What are the weapons of puny man to me?" the Demon answered. "Your weapons will touch me lightly, like leaves falling from the trees."

"I have warned you," the young man said. He took a poisoned arrow from his quiver, placed it in his bow, and shot it at the Demon's heart.

But the arrow caught and dangled in the long blue hair. The Prince shot another arrow, and it too caught in the Demon's hair. A hundred arrows he shot, but none reached the monster's body. The Hairy Demon grinned evilly and began to move toward the Prince. The Raja's son took his war-ax from his belt and struck a mighty blow with it, but the ax became entangled in the hair. He drew his sword and tried to pierce the net of hair, but the sword became entangled and fell from his hand. He took his spear and hurled it, but the spear too was embedded and lost in the hair.

Then the Hairy Demon took hold of the Raja's son with his tiger-like claws, and the young man's shield too became entangled and lost.

"You evil Demon of the Forest," the Raja's son cried out, "do you think I fear you?" He struck the monster a fierce blow with his right hand, but it stuck in the matted hair. He struck with his left hand, and it, too, became stuck in the hair. He kicked a violent blow with his right foot, which became entangled helplessly. And he kicked then with his left foot, and his left foot, too, was snarled in the hair.

"I fear you not!" the Prince shouted, and summoning all his strength, he butted the creature's body with his head. Then he was quite still, for his head was stuck also, and he hung suspended in the air unable to move.

The Hairy Demon spoke, saying: "You have tried to slay me with five weapons, and you have tried to slay me with your body itself. Now you are helpless. Will you now beg for mercy?"

"I cannot fear you," the Raja's son said, "for I do not fear evil in whatever form it appears."

"Your courage is great," the Demon said, "but I am hungry all the same."

"The struggle has not ended," the Prince said. "There is still the sixth weapon."

"I see no weapon," the Demon answered.

"If you eat me, you will feel it," the young man said. "The sixth weapon is a terrible thunderbolt concealed within me. If you eat me, it will destroy you forever."

The Demon paused, saying: "What weapon is this?"

"It is the weapon of Knowledge, which I have within me. Wherever they come together, Knowledge destroys Evil."

And hearing this, the Hairy Demon released the Raja's son and placed him on the ground.

"What you say is true. Go your way in safety. I will trouble you no more."

The Hairy Demon gave the Raja's son his five weapons, the war-ax, the spear, the sword, the shield, and the bow with its arrows. He stood aside as the young man passed and continued his journey to Benares.

And when the Prince arrived in Benares, he told them of the battle. The nature of the sixth weapon, Knowledge, was revealed. With his six weapons the young man became his father's right hand, and at last became the Raja of Benares.

The Man from Kailasa

A TALE FROM SOUTH INDIA

In the State of Madras, in a village called Rasipur, there
lived a landowner named Gopal, who was known by his
neighbors as a man who bargained hard, never gave anything to anyone, and hid his money away as fast as he ac-
cumulated it. But by a strange act of fate, Gopal's wife
was as generous as he was stingy. While Gopal would
strangle himself before he would give a small copper coin
to a beggar, his wife gave too generously and too often. She
was unable to tell the difference between a person who
needed help and a person who was taking advantage of her
simple nature. So willing was she to rush to the aid of the
poor that her reputation spread not only among beggars
and wandering holy men, but among rascals and thieves as
well. Day after day people wandered to her door to ask for
food or alms, and no one ever went away without getting
at least a little of what he had come for.

Though Gopal was rich, his wife's generosity made him
frantic. He scolded, shouted, and threatened to beat her.
She would answer with tears in her eyes that she would
try to do better. But the sight of a beggar always made her
compassionate, and she would go to the place where the
money was hidden and find a few coins for him.

In another village near Rasipur was a man who decided
to swindle Gopal of some of his riches. He came to Rasipur one morning and hid behind some bushes until he saw
Gopal mount his horse and ride away to inspect his fields.
Then the man threw dust on his legs as though he had been

58

on a great journey, and he went in front of Gopal's house and fell on the ground, pretending to be overcome by exhaustion. Seeing the stranger lying there, Gopal's wife rushed out to see what was the matter.

"I am a resident of Kailasa on Shiva's holy mountain, where the dead ancestors reside," the man said. "I was sent down here with a message from an old couple who died and went to Kailasa many years ago. I am looking for their son. But I have walked far and I am worn out, and I doubt that I shall ever find him."

Gopal's wife had tears in her eyes while listening to the man's story.

"Oh," she said, "those dear old people, to think of their son and remember him! What village are you looking for?"

"They said that their son lived in Rasipur."

"Rasipur! Then you have arrived. This is Rasipur. And what is the name of the man?"

"Gopal is his name. He is a landowner in Rasipur," the man replied.

"Oh," the woman cried, "the gods have sent you straight to his house! I am Gopal's wife. How glad my husband would be to see you if he were only here! Tell me about the old people in Kailasa. How are they doing?"

She brought him food to eat while he talked. He said:

"Kailasa is a beautiful place to be in if one only has the necessities of life. Gopal's parents could be happy if only they had enough to eat and decent clothes to cover their bodies."

Again Gopal's wife had tears in her eyes. "Are things going so badly with the dear old people?" she asked.

"Mother," the man said, "it would be difficult to describe to you the miseries they are suffering in the other world. For clothing they are wearing only rags, and for the past six days they have had no food whatever. It would break your heart to see them."

"Why should they suffer so when their son has plenty of everything?" the woman said indignantly. She went into the house and gathered together her best clothes for Gopal's mother. And she made another bundle of Gopal's best clothes for his father. After that she prepared a huge bundle of food. She gave them to the man, saying: "Hurry, take these things back to Kailasa for the good old people!"

The man answered: "Yes, they will be grateful for these little gifts. But the old lady, shouldn't she have some jewelry to adorn herself with?"

"Yes, how thoughtless of me!" Gopal's wife answered. She then brought out her own jewelry and pressed it into the hands of the unscrupulous man.

Nervous that Gopal might return before he had gotten safely away, the thief promised to deliver everything into the hands of the old people before nightfall, and hurried away. As soon as he was out of sight of the house, he began to run.

Just at this moment Gopal returned and dismounted from his horse. His wife's pleasure at the kindness she had just done was so great that she rushed out to meet him. She told him about the messenger from Kailasa, and how the old people had sent a message asking for help, and how she had given the man a large bundle for them.

Gopal stood speechless, with his mouth open, while his wife described the clothing and jewels she had sent. He felt weak. A chill went through his body. Then he became hot with rage. Without another word to his wife he mounted his horse and galloped off in pursuit of the thief.

Thinking that Gopal merely had more news to send his parents, his wife waved her arms and pointed, shouting. "That way, that way! The messenger went in that direction!"

After riding several miles, Gopal saw the man on the road ahead of him. The thief, seeing that he was pursued

and that the horse would soon catch up to him, tied his loot over his shoulder and climbed a tall tree by the road-side. Gopal rode his horse under the tree and shouted: "Come down, you rascal! I have caught you! Come down!"

But the thief was terrified. He replied: "No, I am sorry; I can't come down. This is the way to Kailasa; I am returning."

"When I catch you, you will certainly go to Kailasa," Gopal shouted. He dismounted from his horse and began to climb the tree after the man, who edged his way out on a limb. When Gopal was thoroughly entangled in the leaves and branches, the thief dropped to the ground, mounted the horse, and rode away.

Gopal came down slowly. He stood watching the thief disappear on his horse. And when at last the horse and rider were out of sight, Gopal began to walk home, cursing his stupidity in having lost his good horse in addition to everything else. As he approached his house, he saw his wife standing at the roadside waiting for him. He couldn't think of a thing to say to her about the missing horse, so he said nothing.

But his wife ran forward and took his hand, saying: "Just as I thought, you good, kind man! What a generous husband you are! Don't say a word; I know what happened. You gave your fine horse to the messenger to take to Kailasa for your father!"

"Yes," Gopal said, wetting his lips with his tongue. "Yes, that is the way it was. Father always preferred to ride. I thought he would be pleased. How nice to think of him dressed in my best clothes, riding about on my horse!"

Thus it is. There are some people in the world who don't willingly give anything away. But when through accident or stupidity they lose something, they pretend to have given it with an open heart.

Krishna the Cowherd

A HINDU EPIC TALE

In the kingdom ruled by the evil King Kansa, a child was born to Vasudeva and Devakee, and his name was Krishna. As Kansa was a demon disguised in human form, Krishna was a god in human form.

It had been foretold by the sages that a child of Devakee would rise up and destroy King Kansa, and so it was that Kansa came to kill the child Krishna. But his parents secretly sent the infant to a distant place, in the care of a cowherd named Nanda and his wife Yashoda. There he lived in safety along with the child Balarama, who was born on the same day at the same hour, in the house of Nanda and Yashoda, in a town called Braja.

Nanda had many cattle. When he went out to herd them and milk them, Yashoda watched over Krishna and Balarama.

Once when the infant Krishna was sleeping, Yashoda placed him under a great ox cart in the shade and went to the river to bathe. While she was gone, Krishna awakened and cried for food. He kicked his legs against the ox cart and shattered its wheels, so that it fell in pieces. When Yashoda returned and saw what had happened, she was frightened and took Krishna in her lap, but he was laughing. Nanda came back from the fields and saw the broken cart and the broken milk jars lying on the ground. He said to Yashoda: "How was the cart broken? Were the bulls fighting?"

And Yashoda said: "I went to the river to wash, leaving Krishna under the cart. When I returned, the cart was broken. I don't know how it happened."

Then some boys came running to Nanda's house. They said: "We saw the baby Krishna lying under the cart. He awoke and kicked the cart over, breaking it to pieces." Hearing this, Nanda and Yashoda were silent. They wondered how such a thing could happen.

Krishna and Balarama were the same size, and they resembled each other as twins. Together they learned to crawl about on the ground. They played childish pranks together, and as they grew, their mischief grew.

One day, exasperated by Krishna's antics, Yashoda tied him by a rope to a great millstone and went inside the house to do her work. When she was gone, Krishna began to crawl, dragging the huge millstone behind him. So heavy was the stone that it gouged up the earth, but still Krishna crawled. He passed between two arjuna trees, and the millstone caught there. Still Krishna continued crawling, dragging the stone, and the stone tore up the arjuna trees by the roots, and they fell with a great crash.

The women of the village came running. They saw Krishna standing among the branches of the fallen trees, laughing. They asked each other: "How could this thing happen? There was no storm to knock down the trees. Neither were elephants rubbing against them." Nanda and Yashoda took Krishna home. They were greatly perplexed.

Krishna and Balarama grew and played together. When they were seven, they were allowed to take the cattle to the grazing fields. With small drums and flutes they played music, and went from field to field with the cattle, enjoying themselves.

One day Krishna said to his companion: "Why do our people continue to live here? The cattle have eaten the grass, the fields are dried up, and men have cut away all the trees. Brindabana on the banks of the Yamuna River is a lovely country with green fields, streams, and ponds on all sides. We should all go to Brindabana. Let us think of a way to make the people of Braja leave this place."

As he said these words, hundreds of dreadful vultures appeared in the sky. They swarmed over the village and the fields, attacking the women and the children and the cattle. The people were terrified. No one dared to go out to the river for water or move anywhere outside their houses. So the people of Braja met together and decided to take what they could carry and go to the wooded land called Brindabana on the banks of the Yamuna River. They built new houses in Brindabana, and the cattle grazed in fresh grass, and there was much fruit from the fruit trees. The people of Braja were happy there.

It happened once that Krishna strolled along in the forest, and he came to the edge of a large lake. Though it was deep and calm, there were no water birds there, and no animals of any kind roamed along its shore. Though it was beautiful, it was desolate as a desert, and Krishna wondered why this should be. Then he remembered that it was the home of the huge serpent Kaleeya, who once had lived in the ocean and had been exiled to this place by the great bird Garuda, enemy of serpents. Because Kaleeya lived and reigned here, people and animals feared to come near, for Kaleeya struck terror into their hearts.

Krishna thought that it was his duty to punish the serpent and make the place safe for the people of Braja. So he climbed a Cadamba tree that stood at the edge of the water, and from its high branches he leaped into the deep lake. A fountain of water rose at the spot where the god Krishna fell, and the lake's surface, calm and quiet before, boiled and surged with waves. Enraged that he had been disturbed, Kaleeya the serpent left his resting place and threw himself upon Krishna. He coiled about the shepherd boy and shot poison out of his five mouths. Other snakes of the lake also took hold of Krishna and tried to kill him. Some cowherds heard the noise, and they came to the lake to see what was happening. They hurried back to the village, shouting: "Krishna has fallen into the lake and is being destroyed by the monster Kaleeya!" The people came to the lake, and Nanda and Yashoda wept.

But Krishna's companion Balarama called out: "Oh, Krishna! The people who are lamenting your fate are merely human beings, and they think you are human like them! Do not distress them any longer! Punish the serpent at once!"

Hearing this, Krishna, who had not struggled yet against the serpents, took hold of their bodies with his hands and freed himself easily. He grasped the hood over the monstrous head of Kaleeya and bent it back; then he stood upon it and danced there. Kaleeya, the huge serpent, was humbled. He said: "Oh, Krishna, I did not recognize you. Take pity on me and do not destroy me."

Krishna said: "I will not destroy you. But I cannot permit you to remain any longer in this lake to poison it and terrorize the people. Take your family and all the serpents that live with you back to the ocean. Let the water of this lake become pure. I know that the Garuda bird is in the ocean and that you fear him. Show him the footprints of my feet on your hood, where I have danced, and he will no longer torment you." Then Kaleeya and his serpents came out of the lake and went to the ocean.

As for Krishna, he stood at the edge of the lake unmarked by the battle, and the herdsmen surrounded him and sang. They said to Nanda: "What glory is yours to have such a child! We know that from this day on Krishna will help us in all our difficulties." So the water of the lake became pure; the people came back to it, and the water birds returned, and the cattle grazed once more along its shores.

There was peace in Brindabana then. Krishna and Balarama again took care of the cattle and joined in the games of the herdsmen. But there was a demon by the name of Pralamba who wished to kill the two companions. He took on the form of a young cattle herder and joined the games of the boys and the young men. He watched Krishna and Balarama closely, waiting for an opportunity to strike them. After a while he decided that Krishna was too strong for him, and he turned his mind to the destruction of Balarama.

One day when the cowherds were having foot races, Pralamba the demon contrived to run against Balarama. The two of them ran with great speed toward a distant tree, and while they ran, Pralamba seized Balarama and put him on his shoulder. But Balarama was heavier than Pralamba supposed, so the demon expanded his body; he grew until he became as large as a full-grown spreading fig tree. He looked like an enormous black cloud moving across the land, with Balarama resting on his back.

Balarama cried, "Oh, Krishna, what shall I do?"

Krishna knew better than Balarama himself the strength that Balarama had within him, and he called back: "Oh, Balarama, because you have a human form, do not deceive yourself! Your power is great; you have the strength of the gods within you! Strike the demon with your fist!"

At these words, Balarama struck a blow like a thunderbolt on Pralamba with his hand, and the demon fell dead upon the ground. Thus Balarama's fame, like Krishna's, spread among men.

A time came when Krishna asked the old cattle herders: "Why do you make great festivals for the god Indra each year?"

The old men said: "We will tell you the reason. The god Indra is great. He rules over the clouds. When he commands them, they shower rain over the earth. The rain makes the grass and the corn grow, and this is the food of our cattle. As Indra is the lord of the clouds, we hold festivals and sacrifices in his honor."

Krishna said to them: "We are milk farmers, and we live in the woodlands and the grasslands. The hills of Brindabana on which the grass and the forests grow are dear to us, and it is the hills that we should worship. We are cradled in the hills; therefore we should praise them and hold festivals in their honor. As for Indra, let others worship him."

And so Krishna persuaded the people to hold a festival in honor of the hills. They put aside their preparations to worship Indra. They decorated their cattle with garlands of flowers and led them out to the hills. Krishna, through his mystic powers, transformed himself into a hill, and the cowherds worshiped him.

When the god Indra saw that people no longer worshiped him, he became angry. He called the clouds together and ordered them to pour rain on Brindabana. The clouds massed, darkness came, lightning flashed in the gloom, and rain and hail fell. For many days the rain came down. The rivers swelled and overflowed, the grassland was flooded, and the cattle began to die. Krishna saw that ruin and death faced the people because of Indra's anger.

To save them, he decided to raise the hill of Govarndhana so that they could find shelter beneath it. He went to the hill and raised it from the ground. He stood in the center and pushed it upward with one arm, calling the people to come into the shelter he had created for them. They came with all their possessions and their cattle, and found dry places for themselves under the hill. The rain came down in great fury, but the people were dry and safe.

Seeing this great accomplishment of Krishna's, the god

Indra withdrew the clouds. The sky became clear, and the sun shone again. The cattle came out of the shelter and grazed, and the people returned to their homes. Then Krishna set the hill down and went to his house.

Many such feats did Krishna do, and he destroyed many demons.

Now the evil King Kansa, who was a demon in disguise, heard of these things and was afraid, because it had been foretold that Krishna, the child of Vasudeva and Devakee, would kill him. So he plotted to destroy Krishna and his companion Balarama. He sent a messenger to bring the two young men to the city of Mathura.

Krishna and Balarama went to the city of Mathura. It was at the time of a great festival in honor of a wonderful archery bow that was kept in the palace. Few men were strong enough to string the bow, and once strung, few men could bend it. Some of the gods, including Indra himself, had been able to bend the bow, but no one had been able to break it. Krishna and Balarama went to the keeper of the bow, asking to see the wonderful weapon. Krishna took it and strung it. Then he pulled on the string. The bow bent, then broke with a noise like thunder, making the earth shake. Krishna put the broken weapon down, and the two companions quickly left.

When the evil Kansa heard what had happened, he was angry and frightened. He sent for the keeper of the royal elephants. He said: "Take the wild and powerful elephant Kuvalayapeeda to the entrance of the arena where the wrestlers and archers will meet tomorrow. When Krishna and Balarama enter, drive the elephant so that he will attack them and destroy them. If they are not killed, surely I will come to my end."

He sent then for the great wrestlers Chanura and Musthika. Like Kansa, they were demons in human form. He said: "You are great wrestlers; there is no one to equal you.

Tomorrow you will wrestle two cowherds from Braja. Though they are young, they are master athletes. Show them no mercy. When you beat them to the ground, you must then kill them."

The wrestlers replied: "Oh King, if the cowherds fight with us, then we will kill them."

The day of the festival came, and the people of Mathura crowded into the arena. Near the gates the wild elephant Kuvalayapeeda waited, and when Krishna and Balarama entered, he rushed at them madly, his trunk raised and his huge tusks thrust forward. Krishna smiled. He grasped the trunk of the onrushing beast and moved under his belly. He twisted the trunk and the elephant fell on his knees. With a blow of his hand he killed Kuvalayapeeda and pulled out his great tusks. The blood of the elephant still on his arms, Krishna went into the festival grounds with Balarama. He moved back and forth like a victorious lion, and the sight of him filled Kansa's heart with malice.

Kansa then ordered the wrestling matches to begin, and he announced that Krishna would fight Chanura, while Balarama would fight Musthika.

Krishna said: "I am young, while Chanura is mature and bulky as a hill. Nevertheless, I will join him in this contest. I will do nothing that is unworthy or unfair. Yet it is clear that Chanura is preparing to injure and kill me. Therefore, the responsibility for what happens is not mine."

The two wrestlers moved toward one another. When one attacked, the other defended himself with skill. Both were agile and fierce. First one was on top, then another. A cloud of dust arose from under their feet, and the ground shook. Nevertheless, Krishna was only playing with Chanura.

As Kansa watched, his heart grew heavy, for he seemed to understand that his days were numbered. At the sight of Krishna, radiant as the sun, performing in the arena, the crowd grew excited. Kansa ordered the palace musicians to stop playing their instruments. But music came down from the skies instead, for the gods had gathered there unseen to watch this contest.

When Krishna was through playing gently with his opponent, he took another form, that of the terrible Krishna the Avenger. And he struck Chanura a fierce blow, and Chanura fell down and died.

Kansa was silent. He watched gloomily as Balarama wrestled with Musthika and killed him also.

When the second of his fighters was dead, Kansa went wild with fear and hatred. He shouted: "Throw out those ignorant cowherds from the arena! Take their guardian Nanda and put him in chains! Krishna's father Vasudeva, seize him and punish him! Send out soldiers to Brindabana to take away all the cattle of Krishna's people!"

Krishna listened with indignation to the cruel orders of King Kansa. Again assuming his terrible form of the Avenger, Krishna leaped upon the platform, caught Kansa by the hair, and destroyed him.

Then he went upon his knees to greet Vasudeva and Devakee, the parents whom he had not seen since he was born.

The Scholars and the Lion

AN INDIAN TALE

There were once four men who were friends. Three of them were wise and learned in books. But the fourth was not a scholar. All he had was common sense.

It happened once that the four men were conversing together. They spoke of how nice it would be to travel to far-off places and see something of the world. "What good are books if we don't go places and apply our learning to the things around us?" one of them said. "Yes," the others said, "the learning we have acquired is much too great to be applied to this little village."

So they prepared themselves with clothes and food and began their journey. And after a while, when they were trudging along the road, one of the three learned men declared:

"I have been thinking. Three of us have spent our lives in study. We have pored through books. We have sat up late at night, reading by the light of our oil lamps until our eyes have closed with weariness. Now we are going out into the world to make our knowledge useful. With the things we have learned we will become rich. Yet there is a fourth man with us, our unlearned friend. Has he studied and prepared for this day? No, he contributes nothing at all to our expedition. Why should he come along and share our hard-earned good luck?"

The second scholar thought and answered: "These are wise and just words." He turned to the unlearned man

72

and said to him: "Good friend, you are no scholar. Please leave us and go home."

The third scholar spoke. He said: "No, this isn't right. He is no scholar, as we all know. But he has been our friend since childhood. Let him come and share with us the great treasures we are going to discover through our wisdom."

They finally decided that their unlearned friend could come along and share with them, even though he had nothing at all to contribute but common sense.

The four men resumed their journey, traveling from place to place in search of wealth and fortune. They passed through a forest, and came to a clearing where the bones of a dead lion were scattered on the ground. They stood looking at the bones of the dead animal. One of the scholars said:

"See what a wonderful opportunity lies here before us. With these bones we can test the value of our learning. Isn't our great scholarship able to bring this creature back to life? For my part, I can assemble the bones of the animal, each in its right place."

The second scholar said: "I too have learning on this subject. I can cover the bones with flesh, blood, and skin."

And the third scholar said: "As for me, I can give this creature life and make it breathe."

The fourth man, who was no scholar at all, was humble and silent before such tremendous learning.

So the first scholar assembled the bones of the lion and put them together. The second scholar put a covering of flesh and skin over the lion, and put blood in the body. Then the third scholar began the business of bringing the lion to life.

At this moment the fourth man, the fellow without any learning in his head, protested vigorously. He said:

"My dear friends, think what you are about to do! This

animal that you are bringing back to life is a lion! If you are successful, he will rise up and kill us all!"

The third scholar, busily applying all his hard-won knowledge, shouted: "What good is learning if it isn't applied to things?"

"I plead with you, think again!" the fourth man said. "But if you are really determined to go through with it, at least wait until I have climbed a tree!"

He scurried up a tall tree and sat in the branches. Then the third scholar resumed his work of bringing the dead lion to life, while the two other scholars stood close by, observing everything he did with the greatest of interest. The third scholar stepped back in triumph.

"It is done!" he exclaimed proudly.

The lion opened its eyes, switched its tail nervously, and got to its feet. And then without warning, it sprang upon the three learned men and killed them.

The fourth man, the one who had never studied books, waited in the tree until the lion had gone away. Then he came down and returned alone to his village.

And so it is that people say:

> *"Scholarship's no substitute for common sense*
> *Attain, if you can, intelligence.*
> *Three senseless scholars lost in pride*
> *Made a lion—then they died."*

The Traveler and the Nut Tree

A KASHMIRI TALE

One day a discontented man was sitting under a nut tree thinking how hard life was and how difficult it was to get along in the world. On the ground near the tree was a pumpkin vine, and on the vine was a large pumpkin.

"Just see how foolish God was when He created things," the man said aloud. "Had God been more clever, we would have no misery in the world. Here is a large strong tree with hundreds of tiny nuts growing on it. And just look at that weak little vine crawling along the ground with an immense pumpkin attached! What a ridiculous mistake God made! It should have been the other way around. The small nuts should be growing on the weak vine, and the big pumpkins should be growing on the strong tree. If it had been arranged that way, instead of the way it is, I would have more respect for the Almighty's wisdom."

As the man finished speaking, a nut fell from the tree and landed squarely on his head. Startled, he looked up into the tree and pondered a moment. Then he said fervently:

"Oh God, forgive me! If one of those big pumpkins had fallen on my head from the top of this tree, it would have killed me! Great is your wisdom!"

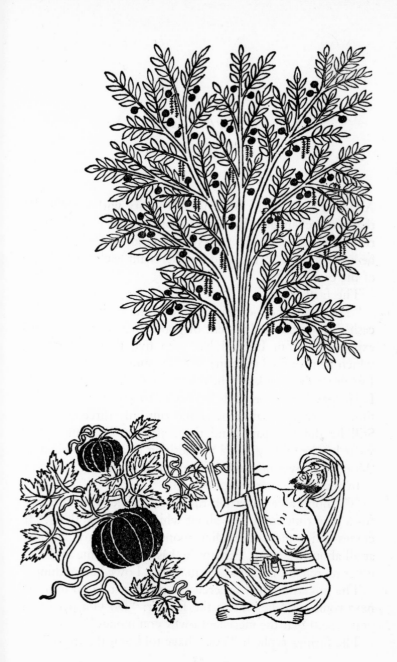

The Debt

A KASHMIRI TALE

A farmer came to the governor of the city with a complaint that a merchant had borrowed money from him and now refused to repay the debt. So the governor ordered a trial to be held, and the farmer and the merchant each told his side of the case.

The farmer said:

"This man, the merchant, came to me saying he needed cash to purchase a shipment of goods that had arrived unexpectedly from India. I lent him five thousand rupees, which he promised to return in a few months. At first when I went to him to ask for the money he said: 'In a few weeks I will pay.' After a while he began to say it was not five thousand rupees that he owed me, but only three thousand. Still he did not pay. And then, after more than a year went by, he said he owed me nothing at all. Now he says: 'Money? I never borrowed money from you.'"

In reply, the merchant declared:

"Oh honorable governor, this man has been hounding me for a long time for a debt about which I know nothing. He comes and comes, demanding money, but I know nothing at all about his claim. Perhaps he has confused me with another merchant. Perhaps he is mad. But I owe him nothing."

The governor then ordered the merchant to go into the next room, and he said to the farmer: "Do you persist in your claim that the merchant owes you money?"

The farmer replied: "Yes, I have told you the truth."

The governor took a knife from the silver sheath he wore and handed it to the farmer, saying: "Then take this knife into the next room where the merchant waits, and cut off his ear. This is my judgment. It is in your favor."

But the farmer answered: "Honorable governor, if you will forgive me, I will not carry out your judgment. I will drop my complaint against the man. Though I came with an honest case against the merchant, I don't care so much for money that I would deprive a man of his ear for it." He laid the knife on the table.

So the governor sent the farmer into the next room and called the merchant before him again.

"I have heard both sides of the case," he said, "and I have weighed it carefully. Do you still claim that you owe nothing at all to the farmer?"

"Yes, it is just as I told you," the merchant said. "The man has made a false claim against me and caused me great inconvenience."

"Then I decide in your favor," the governor said. "Take this knife, go into the next room, and cut off the farmer's ear."

The merchant took the knife and started for the next room. As he was about to pass through the door, the governor called him back.

"I now have the correct answer to the case," he said. "I rule that the farmer has won. You are hereby ordered to pay the man his five thousand rupees. Tell me no more lies. A man that would cut off a fellow man's ear for a sum of money is not to be trusted. This is my judgment."

The Boy and the Cloth

A KASHMIRI TALE

A poor woman sent her son to market with some cloth she had woven and instructed him to sell it for four rupees. The boy went and sat down in front of the bazaar with the cloth, waiting for someone to come and buy it. A man stopped and looked at the cloth and saw that it was very good.

"I'll give you six rupees for the cloth," he said.

"Don't be silly," the boy said, "that's not the price."

"Very well, I'll give you seven then," the man said.

"No," the boy said firmly, "there is only one price I'll accept. There's no need to try to bargain with me."

"What are you asking for the cloth?" the man replied.

"Four rupees. If you don't give me four rupees for it, you are a scoundrel."

The man was angry at being called a scoundrel, and he supposed the boy was trying to make a fool out of him. He scolded the boy for his insolence and went away.

When the boy got home, he told his mother he hadn't sold the cloth.

"I almost sold it," he said, "but the man didn't want to give me four rupees; he wanted to give me seven. I refused and called him a scoundrel."

"Oh! Oh!" the woman moaned. She upbraided the boy for not knowing that seven is more than four. "And never call people scoundrels," she said. "Be polite to people.

Salaam to everyone. If you had salaamed to the man in the market, he wouldn't have gone away angry."

She sent him back to market the next day with the cloth. Remembering her advice, the boy salaamed to everyone he passed on the road. When there were no people passing, he salaamed to houses, to trees, and to horses. A man went by driving several donkeys ahead of him. The boy salaamed to the donkeys. This made the driver angry. He cried out:

"Whatever are you doing? When we are dealing with donkeys, we don't salaam them; we say *fri fri* to make them move along!"

The boy remembered what the donkey driver had told him. He came to where a man had a snare set to catch some birds. A bird was just getting ready to enter the snare. But the boy shouted *fri fri* at the bird, and it flew away.

The owner of the snare was angry, and he shouted:

"You're not supposed to say *fri fri* to the birds! You're supposed to say *lag lag!*" Those were the words a person said when he wanted the birds to come and be caught.

As the boy walked along, he encountered two thieves escaping from a garden where they had been stealing fruit.

"*Lag lag!*" the boy called out.

"What are you saying?" one of the thieves warned. "Be quiet or say something else. Go and say, 'Let go of this one and take another.'" And they ran away.

So the boy stood in the street and shouted: "Let go of this one and take another!"

Just then a funeral passed by. People were carrying a coffin to the cemetery.

"Let go of this one and take another!" the boy called out.

"Be quiet," the mourners told him. "Don't you have any respect for the dead?"

So the boy became quiet then, not knowing what else to say. When he came at last to the market place, he saw a goldsmith at work. He saw how the goldsmith put his golden ornaments into the fire to process them. And he saw how people came and bought the things the smith took out of the fire.

"So this is the secret!" the boy said. "I never knew how it was done!"

He took his cloth and threw it into the goldsmith's fire, saying: "Now someone will buy it."

But in a moment there wasn't anything left of it but ashes.

The Wrestler of Kyushu

A JAPANESE TALL TALE

There was a wrestler who lived on the southern island of Kyushu. He was a champion of Sumo wrestlers and known to be very strong as well as skillful. He had many contests and he was always the winner. But in defeating his opponents, he never had to use all of his great strength.

One day this wrestler was walking alone through the countryside looking at the wild flowers and trees. He came to the edge of a river and stood watching the water flow quietly along and listening to the sounds of birds and frogs.

As he stood there, he noticed a movement in the water, and a wave came rolling in and washed up on the sand against his feet. A snake's head emerged from the water, and the snake looked quietly at the wrestler for several minutes. The wrestler, in turn, watched the snake. The two of them stared at each other without moving.

After a while the snake made motions with his head, looking back toward the middle of the river, as though inviting the wrestler to enter or to cross to the other side. But the wrestler had no notion of going into the river or of crossing it. He stood motionless.

When some time went by, the snake withdrew its head into the water. Again there were waves, and now the snake's tail came out of the river. The tail came out further and further, moving up on the bank to the place where the wrestler stood. Still the man did not move. The tail wrapped around

83

one of the wrestler's legs and pulled. When the wrestler felt this tugging, he braced his feet wide apart as though he were in a Sumo contest. Although the snake pulled with great force, the wrestler did not budge. The tail uncoiled and wrapped several times around the other leg, from the man's knee to his ankle, and again it began to pull. The wrestler smiled, and said politely: "I do not wish to come. I stood here peacefully on this shore to breathe in the smell of wild fruit blossoms. Do you not understand that raw force cannot win over the science of Sumo?"

The wrestler dug his feet into the ground and gripped the earth with his toes. The snake pulled fiercely. The water in the middle of the river churned and boiled from the thrashing of the snake's body beneath the surface, and the coils around the wrestler's leg tightened like bands of iron. The wrestler hardened his muscles. Though the pulling was the most powerful force the wrestler had ever encountered, he dug his toes deeper into the earth and braced himself, and he did not move an inch from the spot where he stood.

The tail of the snake became tense and rigid like a tree, the water was covered with waves and whitecaps, and then the body of the snake snapped and broke in two. The contest was over. The wrestler of Kyushu unwrapped the tail from around his leg and went home.

He sent his servants to the river to bring out the body of the snake and measure it. They found the tail where the contest had taken place and pulled it from the water. It was thirty feet long, and where the body had snapped in two it was three feet thick. At first they searched in the river for the other half of the snake, but they did not find it. Then they found it on the opposite shore, wrapped around a large oak tree. This half also was thirty feet long. Even though it had been anchored to the sturdy tree, the snake had not been able to move the wrestler from where he stood.

There was awe and wonder in Kyushu when the news of the contest was heard. And people said: "How strong this man is! He has the strength of many men!"

The wrestler then had a rope made, exactly the size of the snake. It was sixty feet long and three feet thick in the middle. He fastened one end to his leg, and ten men pulled on the other end without moving him. Then fifty men tried, then a hundred. And when one hundred and thirty men pulled together, the wrestler felt his feet move a little.

Thus it was known that the wrestler of Kyushu was as strong as one hundred and thirty men. So it is said.

The Counting of the Crocodiles

A JAPANESE TALE

On the Island of Oki, in ancient times, there lived a hare who longed to go to the mainland to live a better life, for the Island of Oki was small and life there was very boring. The hare often sat on the beach looking longingly across the stretch of water that separated him from what he thought was surely paradise.

One day while he sat there a crocodile poked his head out of the water and looked hungrily at the hare.

"Why do you look at the king of the hares in this manner?" the hare said. "Have you no manners?"

"King of the hares?" the crocodile replied. "That is laughable."

"Do not expose your ignorance this way," the hare replied. "I have more subjects serving me than there are crocodiles between here and the mainland."

"Such statements are ridiculous," the crocodile said. "Do you have any notion of how many of us there are hidden below the water?"

"Yes, there are only a few compared to the hares."

The crocodile replied angrily: "Oh, stupid hare! If you were to see all those who belong to the crocodile kingdom, you would be overcome with terror!"

"Very well, let me see them," the hare said.

So the crocodile went below the water and a few minutes later many crocodiles came to the surface. More and more rose to the top, until the water was covered with them.

The first crocodile appeared again, and said to the hare: "Now you may choke on your words. Have you ever seen so many crocodiles?"

"No," the hare said, "I have never seen so many crocodiles, but still they are not as many as the hares."

"You lie," the crocodile said. "The crocodiles are more numerous!"

"Very well, we shall count," the hare said. "First we shall count the crocodiles, then the hares. Tell your friends to move more closely together so that we may begin."

And when the crocodiles had moved more closely together, the hare jumped on the back of one and called out "One." He jumped on the back of another and called out

"Two." Each number that he called the crocodiles repeated after him. The hare jumped from back to back toward the mainland. "One hundred twenty," he called. "One hundred twenty," the crocodiles answered. When he was near the shore of the mainland, the hare stood on the back of the last crocodile and shouted: "Oh, stupid crocodiles! How vain you are! All you have accomplished is to make a bridge for me to the mainland!" Then he leaped for the land, but the last crocodile, hearing the insulting words, snapped his jaws and bit off the hare's tail.

Though the hare was safe, he had lost his tail by talking too soon. Thus it is that the hare has only the stump of a tail today, whereas once it was long and bushy.

Abunuwas the Trickster

TALES FROM ARABIA

Of all men who lived in ancient times, Abunuwas was the greatest joker that people remember. He was known in every corner of Bagdad, and even Harun-al-Rashid, the ruler of the city, listened to stories of this man's exploits with great amusement. Whoever tried to outjoke Abunuwas played a dangerous game, for Abunuwas's wit and humor knew no limits. When it was in his mind to make a clever person look less clever, or to make people laugh, he spared neither the farmer nor Harun-al-Rashid himself.

It is said that one day Abunuwas was drinking in a coffee shop with friends, and one of his friends declared: "I wish that God would give me a hundred dinars. I can think of many ways to spend so much money."

Another friend laughed and answered: "Why just a hundred dinars? While you are wishing, wish for two hundred."

"What plain fellows you are!" Abunuwas said. "You have no imagination. If God wants to be good, he can be very good. As for me, I wouldn't settle for less than a thousand dinars. If God were to offer me a thousand, I would accept it. If He were to offer me nine hundred ninety-nine, I would refuse it."

News of Abunuwas's boast went around the coffee shops and bazaars of Bagdad, and people asked each other: "Is Abunuwas so arrogant that he would refuse God's gift of nine hundred ninety-nine dinars and demand a full thousand?"

A rich merchant of Bagdad who heard of Abunuwas's boast decided he would put the matter to a test. In the dark of night he placed a pile of silver coins on the doorstep of Abunuwas's house. In the morning when Abunuwas came out, he found the money there, and he also found a great crowd of people standing around waiting to see what he would do. Abunuwas counted the silver, and as he counted, the crowd watched and counted with him. When the last piece of silver had been accounted for, Abunuwas exclaimed: "Thanks be to God! He has answered my request for money!"

"Wait," the merchant called out. "How much did you ask for and how much did you receive?"

"I requested a thousand dinars," Abunuwas answered, "and God has provided me with nine hundred ninety-nine, only one short of what I asked for. But it doesn't matter; I will lend that one dinar to God. He will give it to me some other time, I am sure, and thus make it an even thousand."

"Just a moment, not so fast," the rich merchant said. "Didn't you boast that if God gave you anything less than a thousand, you would turn it down? You must return the money. It is I who placed it there."

"Oh no," Abunuwas said firmly. "This gift is from God. I prayed to Him for it, and He gave it to me. If He has succeeded in raising nine hundred ninety-nine dinars, surely He will find another dinar somewhere to round out the amount."

The merchant saw that he would have difficulty in getting his money back. He had exposed Abunuwas's boast, but it was turning out badly for him. So he said: "We shall take the matter before Harun-al-Rashid."

"Gladly," Abunuwas replied. "But how can I go before the Caliph in these soiled clothes? Lend me a cloak and a tur-

ban and provide me with a donkey to ride, and I shall go with you."

So the merchant provided Abunuwas with a cloak and a turban from one of his shops, and with a donkey from his own stable, and they rode to the court of Harun-al-Rashid with the crowd at their heels.

Harun-al-Rashid listened to the story of the merchant, and then he asked to hear what Abunuwas had to say. When Abunuwas answered the complaint, he spoke indignantly.

"This man is creating a great deal of trouble," Abunuwas said. "If he can make such an outrageous claim against me as this one, the next thing you know he will be telling you that my turban is his, that the very clothes on my back are his, and that even my poor donkey is his."

"They are indeed!" the merchant said. "The turban, the cloak, and the donkey are mine!"

"You see," Abunuwas said to Harun-al-Rashid. "It is just as I predicted."

When the Caliph heard this, he nodded his head in agreement. It was clear to him that Abunuwas was being abused and slandered by the merchant, and he said that Abunuwas had won the case.

It is told that one time a man came to Abunuwas and asked for the loan of his donkey.

"What a pity!" Abunuwas said. "I would like to help you, but my donkey isn't here today; he has gone on a journey."

The donkey was standing behind the house, out of sight, but just at that moment he brayed loudly. The man was angered at hearing the donkey's voice, and he reproached Abunuwas.

"Wasn't that the bray of a donkey? I thought you said your donkey was away on a journey."

"Now look here," Abunuwas said firmly. "Did you come to borrow a donkey or a bray? The donkey isn't here. But if it's a bray you want I'll let you have one."

So Abunuwas brayed: "Eee-haw! Eee-haw! Eee-haw!"

And he told the startled man: "There is your bray. Climb on it quickly and be on your way."

They say that one day Abunuwas went to the house of his stingy neighbor and asked for the loan of a watering pan for his donkey to drink from. The neighbor was very reluctant, but he searched around until he found a worn and leaky copper pot, and he handed it to Abunuwas, saying: "Here is a pot, but I must have it back within four days."

Abunuwas took the large copper pot home and kept it three days. On the fourth day he put a small pan inside the large pot and carried them to the house of his neighbor.

"Here is the pot I borrowed. I am grateful for your kindness," Abunuwas said.

When the neighbor saw the small pan nestling inside, he said: "Oh, but this small one isn't mine."

"Indeed it is," Abunuwas replied. "What is yours is yours. During the night your large copper pot gave birth to this little one. I found them together in the morning. As the small one is the offspring of the large one, they both belong to you. I am no thief, so what is yours I return."

To himself the neighbor said: "What kind of foolishness is this?" But he saw no reason why he shouldn't profit from

Abunuwas's stupidity, so he replied:

"How true. Since the small one is the child of the large one, they both belong to me. May your house be blessed, for even the pots and pans are fruitful there!"

Some days later Abunuwas again went to the house of his neighbor and asked for the loan of a large pot. This time the neighbor was more than willing. Remembering his happy experience with the old battered pot, he now gave Abunuwas the best copper pot he owned. If this fine pot were to have a child as the other one did, it would be good luck indeed.

Abunuwas thanked him and went away. But this time he didn't return the pot at all. So, after many days went by, the neighbor came to Abunuwas's house and asked for it. Abunuwas looked very sad, almost as though tears were ready to run from his eyes.

"I have bad news for you," he said.

"What is the matter?" the neighbor asked in alarm.

"Your pot is dead," Abunuwas replied.

"What!" the neighbor cried out.

"Yes, I knew it would grieve you; that's why I didn't let you know when it happened."

The neighbor became indignant.

"Abunuwas," he said, "don't try to make a fool out of me. Since when does a copper pot die?"

"Can a pot give birth to a young one?" Abunuwas asked.

"Yes," the man said, thinking how he had gotten a small pan for nothing.

"Surely you know that everything that can produce young must die some day," Abunuwas said. "It is sad that your pot had to die away from home."

His angry neighbor argued, but finally he went away. Abunuwas kept the pot. And everywhere that the story was told, people said:

"Abunuwas is right. Anything that can bring forth children is destined to die."

Even the Caliph Harun-al-Rashid felt the sting of Abunuwas's humor. It is said that one night the Caliph dreamed that there was a treasure buried under the floor of Abunuwas's house. The next morning he sent soldiers to dig the treasure up. Abunuwas wasn't home, and his wife couldn't do anything but protest. The soldiers dug holes in the floor and under the walls, but they didn't find anything, and at last they went away. When Abunuwas returned and saw the holes in the floor and under the walls, he was angry. His wife was in tears.

"Never mind," Abunuwas said. "I will repay the Caliph for this."

He told his wife to cook a pot of rice. When the rice was cooked, Abunuwas placed some of it in a dish and covered it loosely with a napkin. He watched the flies come and settle on the dish, and he saw some of them crawl underneath to get at the rice.

The next morning, without disturbing the napkin, he took the dish of rice and went to Harun-al-Rashid.

"I have a complaint," he told the Caliph. "I accuse certain individuals of coming into my house uninvited and eating my food."

Harun-al-Rashid wasn't sure whether or not Abunuwas was accusing him for having dug up his floors. He said sternly: "Whom are you accusing?"

Abunuwas pulled the napkin off the dish of rice, and three flies flew out.

"These are the ones I accuse," Abunuwas said. "They eat my rice without my permission."

The Caliph smiled.

"You are accusing the flies? What can I do about flies?"

"I want justice," Abunuwas said firmly. "I want the right to punish the flies."

The Caliph was highly amused by the joke. He said: "Very well, I give you the right to punish the flies. Wherever you see a fly has settled, you may strike it." And he wrote his judgment out on a piece of paper and signed it with his name.

Abunuwas made a stick with a heavy knob on the end. Wherever he went, he struck flies with it. If he saw flies on the dates in the market place, he would strike them and scatter the dates in every direction. If he saw flies on the fruit in the shops, he would strike them, smashing the fruit and making it worthless. When the shopkeepers protested, Abunuwas would say: "I do not hit the fruit; I hit the flies," and he would show them the order signed by the Caliph. He went along this way for weeks, and while some people were upset by the foolishness, others thought that it was quite funny. Even Harun-al-Rashid had to laugh when he heard what was going on.

Then one day the Caliph was holding court, and Abunuwas came and sat down nearby. The Caliph was judging a lawsuit, and he was talking earnestly. While he was talking, a fly settled on his back. Abunuwas raised his stick with the heavy knob and struck the Caliph a hard blow. Instantly the court was in wild disorder. Abunuwas was seized by the guards, but he said:

"How can you punish me? I didn't strike the Caliph; I merely struck a fly which sat on his back. Harun-al-Rashid himself gave me permission to do this."

He showed them the order signed by the Caliph. They saw it was true. Harun-al-Rashid himself acknowledged that he had signed the document, and Abunuwas was released.

The tale is told that Harun-al-Rashid determined one

time to make Abunuwas look foolish. He called his secretary and instructed him like this:

"Tell everyone who attends court tomorrow to bring an egg concealed in his clothes. Only Abunuwas must not be told. Everyone will know but he. When the session of the court is finished, I will order everyone present to lay an egg. Everyone will pretend to lay an egg, and only Abunuwas will look silly."

The court convened the next morning, and the Caliph listened to the lawsuits. When the hearings were over, he announced in a stern voice:

"I hereby decree that everyone present in the court shall lay an egg immediately. Anyone who doesn't lay an egg will be thrown into prison."

Instantly there was a cackling all through the court, and in a few minutes everyone except Abunuwas was holding up an egg. Harun-al-Rashid looked at Abunuwas accusingly.

Then Abunuwas jumped to his feet, flapped his arms up and down against his sides, and crowed: "Cock-a-doodle-doo!"

The Caliph looked at him in surprise.

"I am glad so many eggs have been laid," Abunuwas said. "There is a large flock of hens here, but you see, I am the rooster."

There was a great laugh in the court. Soon Harun-al-Rashid himself was laughing. Although the joke had been turned against the Caliph, he ordered that Abunuwas be allowed to go free.

The Spotted Rug

AN ARABIAN TALE

There is a saying among the people, "He has spotted the rug." This expression is heard when a person who has performed a kind service receives bad treatment in return.

It is told that a sudden sickness came to the house of a wealthy merchant. His wife had just given birth to a son, and the mother and the baby were very weak and it looked as though both of them might die.

In the village where they lived there was a hakim, or doctor, and he came to see what he could do. When he had finished making his examination, he said: "For this sickness I have no remedies. But there is a wandering hakim now resting at an oasis three days' ride from here. If your wife and son can be saved, it is this man who knows the secret."

"Let him be sent for at once!" the merchant cried out. "I will pay him anything he asks if he will come and drive away this illness from my house!"

So a messenger was sent to the oasis. He rode three days on a fast-running camel, and when he arrived there, he inquired as to the whereabouts of the doctor of the great reputation. The people pointed to a ragged tent, and in it the messenger found an aged man preparing his coffee.

"Are you the great doctor of whom everyone has heard?" the messenger asked.

"I know not what you have heard," the old man replied simply, "but Allah has given me the gift to help the sick."

The messenger looked at the man's poor and ragged clothes. It seemed impossible that this was the healer he had come so far to find. But he said:

"There is a rich and good merchant in my village. His wife and newborn child have been stricken with a strange sickness, and he needs you."

"Are there no hakims nearby?" the old man said.

"Yes, there is one in our village. But he can do nothing. He has advised us that only you have knowledge of this sickness. The merchant says he will pay you any amount you ask to come and save his family."

"I am not young any more," the old man said. "The ride will be hard, for we must hurry. Yet I will come."

And so he prepared his things and packed them on a camel and began the return journey with the messenger. They rode all day, and as night fell the wind rose and the sand lifted from the floor of the desert and filled the air. For two days the sandstorm blew, and the old doctor and the messenger pressed forward slowly and painfully. Then the storm ended, and the sun shone down hot and pitilessly on the travelers. But at last they reached the village.

The merchant welcomed the old man with tears in his eyes, for his wife and son were truly ill.

For two weeks the aged hakim nursed them, and slowly they regained their health. And then one day another messenger came to the village for the old man, telling of how he was needed elsewhere. Again he mounted his camel, and again he rode away into the desert, not even stopping to ask payment for his work.

As time went on, the merchant's wife was as healthy as ever, and his son thrived. No one would ever have guessed that they had been so close to death. They spoke sometimes of the old doctor who had come out of the desert and then returned to the desert. But little by little they forgot him, and life went on as though he had never existed.

And then one day a bedouin came to the merchant's house.

"I am a friend of the aged hakim who saved your wife and son," the man said. "It is said that you promised him anything he might ask for his services. He is in need now, and begs you to send him a hundred riyals."

"A hundred riyals!" the merchant exclaimed with surprise. "That is a fortune! What does a poor man like him need with a hundred riyals?"

"I know not," the bedouin replied. "I know only that he needs it."

"He performed a service for me, it is true," the merchant said. "But he is dreaming if he thinks this is a fair fee. Look, my wife and child are thriving. Had the old man not come I would certainly have found another. And it is quite likely that he arrived when the sickness was already leaving. Here, take him twenty riyals; he will be satisfied with that."

So the bedouin took the twenty riyals and rode away.

A year passed, and one morning the aged hakim came out of the desert on his camel to the merchant's house. He was more ragged than before, and his long beard was wind-blown and unkempt.

The merchant took him into the house and served him coffee, but he was reluctant in all that he did. He thought: "What will people say, knowing that I am entertaining this ragged and dirty creature?"

They spoke of many things. At last the old man said: "May the grace of Allah be on you for the twenty riyals you sent me."

"Twenty riyals!" the merchant thought. "Could I possibly have sent this man twenty riyals? It should have been ten at the most."

"Yet it was said in the beginning, when I was sent for, that you would pay any amount," the old man said. "I asked only one hundred riyals. As I am in great need now, because of my advancing age, would you give me the eighty pieces that remain?"

"Eighty riyals more!" the merchant exclaimed. "What kind of dream is this? I have never forgotten your services, but there is a limit to all things."

He put his coffee cup on the table and stood up. "There is something I want to show you," he said.

The old man stood up and followed him. The merchant led the way into the room where his wife and child had once lain at the point of death.

"You remember this room? Here you sat on my most precious Persian rug, an heirloom from my father. Here you mixed your medicines. I do not blame you for your shaking hands, for you are an old man. But as you can see, you spilled the medicines on the rug, and they have left stains that none of my servants have been able to remove. No longer is this precious rug perfect and flawless. To the end of time it will be spotted, as it is today. Who can ever recompense me for this loss?"

The aged hakim looked at the rug and smiled.

"Yes," he said, "I understand."

And he went out of the merchant's house, mounted his camel, and rode away into the desert.

This is the story people think about when they feel a good act has been repaid with ingratitude, and they say: "He has spotted the rug."

The Philosophers of King Darius

A TALE FROM IRAN

Darius, the King of Persia, gathered his philosophers together and gave them a question to answer. He said: "What is the most powerful thing in life? What is it that prevails over everything else? To the man that answers this riddle, I will give a belt set with jewels like the one I wear, and a purse filled with gold."

The learned men and the philosophers pondered over this question, and another day they met with Darius to give their answers.

One of them said: "Oh Great King, the strongest thing in life is wine. On all who drink it, it has the same effect. It plays no favorites, but treats kings and beggars alike. It confuses and deludes. When the slave weary of life drinks it, he becomes as happy as though he were a landlord. His master, when he drinks it, is as happy as though he were an emperor. And a king, when he drinks, becomes careless and without worry for the present or the future. Wine makes men forget their families, their poverty, and their ambitions. The servant forgets his orders, and the general of the armies forgets what the king has told him to do. It gives courage to cowardly men, and to weak men it gives the illusion of strength. A strong man when he drinks becomes unable to stand, and an eloquent man finds that his tongue will no longer speak correctly. It is clear that wine is the most powerful thing in life."

Another philosopher then asked for permission to speak. He said: "Oh King, it is not the wine that is most powerful, but man who devised it and drinks it. Man keeps flocks and grows grain so that he and his kind may live, storing food so that in drought or famine he will be safe. He is superior to the animals in all respects. By his hands, stones and bricks are laid one on the other to make walls, houses, and cities. It is the mind of man that dreams up these things before they happen. Without man would we have towns and kingdoms? Doesn't man build the ships that sail where once only monsters of the deep dared go? Man has tamed the wild ox, the sheep, the camel, and the elephant and made them his servants. He preserves the history of his race in poetry and song. He has counted the stars and given them names. Surely there is nothing to exceed man in nature."

A third man spoke, saying: "Oh King, these speakers have spoken well, but there is another thing still greater than wine and men."

"Let us hear your argument," Darius said.

So the man began: "Of all powerful things in our lives, woman is the greatest. She is superior to man. If it were not for woman, there would be no men in the world at all. The mother of the slave, she is a woman. The mother of a king, she is a woman too. Is it not woman who spins and weaves? Is it not woman who cares for the children and sees that her husband is fed and consoled? When a young man leaves the house of his parents, is it not because he has found a woman for his wife? Many a man has given up an inheritance for the sake of a woman. And those who become rich, what do they do with their money? They purchase ornaments and jewels to hang around the necks of their wives. They send to distant lands to buy perfumes and rare silks, all for their wives. If a man insults another, there is bloodshed. But if a woman belittles a man or spurns his affections or speaks harshly to him he crawls away like a beaten dog. Even if a woman strikes a man in love with her, does he strike back? No, he grins like a silly idiot, or else he walks about the streets as though death has struck. Therefore, is not woman the most powerful thing in life?"

Darius said: "Indeed, you have made out a strong case for woman. Is there anything to exceed her?"

Then another speaker declared: "Oh King of Persia, I believe it is true that woman is superior to man, but she is not the greatest. The most powerful thing in life is wealth. Without it, who are we? With gold and silver we buy flocks and land and build our houses. It is money that buys slaves to cut stone and till fields. It is money that pays the blacksmith who forges our weapons of war, so that we may fight against our enemies; without our swords and our chariots we would be swallowed up by the nations that envy and despise us. How would we buy silk and precious oils except by money? Without a little wealth a man could not even find a wife. When a king wishes to gain the favor of a foreign prince, he sends gifts of treasure. And when a king has waged a victorious war, his first act is to seize the treasure of his victims. Without wealth, would our lives be the same?"

When this philosopher was finished, another said: "Gracious ruler, I have listened to the arguments put forward with such enthusiasm. But I disagree with all that has been said, for the greatest power in life is a king. A king governs all things on land and sea. He commands his subjects and they obey. He judges their disputes and they accept his word as final. He gives lands to the people and takes them away; they are dependent on his good will. They bring taxes and offerings to him. They build cities at his command. They go out in armies to fight his enemies, climb fortified walls, and destroy cities. Soldiers go to their death by the tens of thousands because their king has so ordered.

The ships that sail the seas, carrying oils and incense, are in the service of the king. And men who stay at home and till the earth bring a share of their grains and fruits to the king as an offering. Thus I have shown that a king is the most powerful thing in life."

Then the people in the room with Darius felt that the last word had been said, and they began to discuss the arguments that had been heard. Some said: "Wine is the greatest." Others said: "No, a king is greatest." Some said it was wealth, some favored woman, and still others said man was the most powerful.

But then an old man asked for permission to speak. Darius called for silence in the room, and the old man said: "Oh great King Darius, forgive me for speaking now that the debate appears to be over. But I have listened carefully to everything that has been said, and all of the arguments are at fault. The greatest thing in life is none of the things that have been mentioned. It is truth. Truth is the most powerful and durable of all things. It does not discriminate between old and young, or between rich and poor. If a poor man or a king commits a wrong act, the truth about it may be hidden for a while, but a time comes when truth shines with all its brightness. Likewise, when any man performs a good deed, no matter how obscure, it will come to be known. Truth can be silenced briefly, but it cannot be silenced forever. If what is told is false, the shadow of truth will fall upon it and obscure it; but if what is told is true, it will shine more brilliantly with the passage of time. Falsehood may be strong and to be feared, but truth is more powerful, because time after time it has struggled with falsehood, and in the end it is always victorious. The rains may fall and wash away the mountains, the sun may beat down and burn up every living thing, but truth is eternal."

On hearing these words, Darius said: "Need we argue any

further as to these matters? Surely this man is right. Nothing that is known to us is equal in power to truth."

And to the old man Darius awarded the sash set with jewels and the bag of gold, as he had promised.

Dinner for the Monk

A TALE FROM LAOS

Standing by the wall of an ancient monastery, there was a magnificent fig tree heavy with fruit. But the chief monk could not bear to see any of the villagers pick the figs. If a man stopped and looked as though he were about to gather some of them, the monk rushed out and waved him away, saying: "These are my figs." This happened day after day, even though there was so much fruit on the tree that the monk couldn't have eaten it all in a year.

Two country men were talking together one day, and they said: "Surely there must be some way to get a few figs from the greedy old monk." And they devised a plan.

The next morning one of them came to the monastery and said: "Will you let me have a few figs from the beautiful tree that stands there?"

"No, no, that is impossible," the monk said. "I need all the fruit for myself."

"What a pity!" the man said. "We have a great portion of venison curry at home, and we thought that if we had a little fruit to go with it, we could invite you to eat with us."

"Oh," the old monk said, his mouth watering at the thought of curry with meat and fruit. "Under those circumstances you can certainly take a little of the fruit. Where do you live?"

"I live beyond the hill over there," the man said. "I will

come for you when the food is ready." And he filled a basket with figs from the tree and went away.

Then the second man came to the monk, saying: "Could you perhaps spare a few figs from the great tree?"

"No, it is impossible," the monk replied. "There are too few; I cannot spare any of them."

"Oh, I am sorry to hear it," the man said. "We have a great portion of pork curry at home, and we thought that if we could add a little fruit, we would be able to invite you to share it with us."

"Ah," the monk said, "in that case you may have some of the fruit. Where is your house?"

"Over the hill," the man said. "When the sun is setting, I will come for you." He filled a basket with the fruit and went away.

All day the old monk thought with pleasure of the vast amount of curry he was going to eat.

In the evening when the sun was going down, the two country men came together to the monastery. They took the monk by the arms and guided him along the trail.

They came to a fork in the trail, where one path went to the east and one to the west. The first man said: "My house lies along the west trail; come with me now to eat venison curry."

The second man said: "My house is on the east trail; come with me now to eat pork curry."

"No," the first man said, "he wants to start with venison curry," and he pulled the monk in the direction of his house.

"No," the second man said, "he prefers to start with pork curry," and he pulled the monk in the other direction.

"On the contrary," the first man said, "he is coming to my house," and he pulled him the other way.

"Not that trail, this trail," the second man said, jerking the monk back.

They began to argue violently, pulling the monk first

in one direction and then another. "This way!" one cried. "No, that way!" the other shouted. They pushed the monk back and forth. They pulled at his sleeves, twisted him, and disputed. The monk was buffeted here and there like a straw in a windstorm.

"Hold on," he said weakly. "Let us reason this out."

But the country men did not listen. They yanked him from one side to the other until he was weary and sore.

"Stop!" he shouted at last. "I have had enough! I don't want venison curry! I don't want pork curry! I only want to go back to the monastery!" He pulled himself free from the hands of the men and fled down the trail.

As they watched him go, one of the men said: "I am sure he wanted venison curry." And the other said: "On the contrary, I know he preferred pork curry."

Then they went home, each on his own path, to make a meal of figs, for neither one of them had meat of any kind.

The Well Diggers

A JAVANESE TALE

Two men named Guno and Koyo went out one day to dig a well. They selected a good spot on the edge of Koyo's rice field and began to dig. They dug all day, working very hard in the hot sun. First Guno was in the hole digging and passing the dirt up in a basket to Koyo. Then Koyo was in the hole digging and passing the dirt up to Guno.

When evening came and they were ready to quit for the day, Koyo looked at the hole with great satisfaction. But when he saw the pile of dirt standing there in his rice field, he was disturbed.

"What are we going to do with this pile of dirt?" he asked Guno.

Guno shook his head.

"I can't have a pile of dirt in my rice field," Koyo said.

"We'll get rid of it," Guno said helpfully. But he couldn't suggest exactly what to do.

The next morning when the two men met, however, Guno had a big smile on his face.

"I've been thinking all night," he said, "and I have solved the problem of what to do with the dirt."

Koyo was glad. He too had been thinking all night. "What shall we do with it?" he asked eagerly.

"Put it in another hole," Guno said.

Koyo was very pleased with the solution. "Why didn't I think of it myself?" he said.

So instead of continuing with the well, the two men began digging another hole where they could put the dirt that had come out of the well. They dug all morning, and in the afternoon they began carrying the dirt from the pile by the well and throwing it into the new hole. By evening the pile by the well was gone, and the new hole was full. Guno and Koyo were very satisfied with themselves. But as they were about to go home, Koyo's eyes rested on the pile of dirt that had come out of the second hole.

"We solved the really big problem," he said, "but what are we going to do with *this* pile of dirt?"

Guno became very thoughtful. The two of them stood looking at the dirt for a while and then Guno said: "I'll think about it tonight. I'm sure we will find a solution."

And then they went home to eat and rest.

The next morning when they met again Guno was smiling broadly.

"I've been thinking," he said.

"I also have been thinking," Koyo said.

"It is obvious," Guno said, "that we merely have to put this dirt in a hole, just as we did with the first pile."

"Ho, why didn't I think of it myself?" Koyo replied. And they started to dig furiously in the middle of Koyo's rice field. First one would stand in the hole passing the dirt up in a basket, then the other would take his turn.

When they thought the hole was large enough, they went to the pile of dirt that had worried them so much and began throwing it into the new excavation. When night came the second pile, at last, was safely in the ground. But Koyo had an anxious expression on his face. He kept looking at the new pile of dirt that had come out of the third hole.

"We are confronted with a new problem, my friend," he said. "We have another pile of dirt to dispose of."

The two of them stood frowning and thinking.

"There must be an answer," Guno said. "Let us sleep on it."

So the two men went home to bed. They were sleepless. They tossed and worried all night. But when Guno arrived in the rice field for work the next morning, he had a happy look on his face.

"We made a mistake in our calculations," he announced. "The third hole was too small! Today we'll dig a hole *twice as large* as the others. Then there'll be room for the dirt from *both* holes!"

As the meaning of Guno's inspiration became clear to him, Koyo too broke out in smiles.

"Why didn't we think of it before?" he said.

And once more they began to dig, this time with great enthusiasm. The new hole was wider than the others and deeper. At last Koyo declared: "It is large enough. It is finished."

Then they began moving the dirt from the previous pile and throwing it into the new hole. When it was all gone, they saw there was still room in the hole for more.

"You see?" Guno cried out triumphantly.

And they commenced to dump in the dirt from the last pile. But in a little while the hole was full, and there still remained a large mound of dirt.

They sat down wearily to think about it, wondering what had gone wrong. Neither of them spoke for a long time. At last Koyo said with resignation:

"Luck is against us. There is only one solution to this terrible problem. Let's throw this dirt into the hole we dug for the well; then there'll be no dirt left to worry about."

And that is what they did.

Guno and Koyo and the Kris

A JAVANESE TALE

One day the two friends Guno and Koyo were traveling from Jenu to Tuban. As they walked along the dusty road, they saw a glittering object lying on the ground. Each of them rushed forward to pick it up, and they saw it was a fine kris, or knife, encased in a silver scabbard.

"What a beautiful kris!" Guno said. "I will sell it in town and be very rich."

"You mean I will sell it," Koyo answered. "Wasn't it I who saw it first?"

"No, on the contrary, it was I," Guno said.

They argued for a while, until at last they agreed they would share their new-found wealth.

When night came, they found a place to rest near the seashore. They placed the kris on the ground between them and went to sleep.

After a while Guno woke up and saw that Koyo was sleeping. He thought: "Didn't I see the kris first? Why should I share it with Koyo?" Very quietly he arose, picked up the kris, and looked for a place to hide it. First he put it under a rock, but he wasn't satisfied. It would be the first place Koyo would look for it. Then he thought of the sea, so he walked out into the water until it was up to his chest. He dropped the kris and dug it into the sand with his toes. After that he came out of the water and lay down and went to sleep.

But Koyo was restless. He woke up and thought:

118

"Wasn't it I who found the kris? Why should I share it with Guno?" He reached out for the kris and discovered it was missing. "Ah, that Guno!" he said. "What has he done with it?" He got up and looked under the rocks nearby. Then he came back and looked at Guno. Just then the moon came out from behind a cloud, and he saw water glistening on Guno's body. "Aha! He has been in the sea!" Koyo said to himself, and he knew then where the kris was to be found.

He got down on his hands and knees and licked Guno's ankles. They were salty. He licked Guno's knees. They were salty. He licked Guno's back. It was salty. When he came to the chest, however, there was no salt taste to it, so Koyo knew how far Guno had walked into the water. He went into the water himself until it was up to his chest. He poked around with his toes until he located the kris. He brought it back, wondering what to do with it.

He saw a field with strawstacks standing in it. He crawled into one of the strawstacks with the kris and went to sleep.

When morning came, Guno awoke and saw that Koyo was missing. He went out into the water and found that the kris too was gone. His eyes fell upon the strawstacks, and he guessed that Koyo was hiding in one of them. There were buffalo grazing in the field, and Guno took the bell from one of them and hung it around his own neck. He got down on his hands and knees and went from one strawstack to another. When he came to a strawstack, he would bump it with his head as though he were a buffalo, and the bell would tinkle. He came at last to the strawstack where Koyo was hiding. He bumped his head into the straw and the bell tinkled. Inside the stack, Koyo thought it was a buffalo eating up his hiding place, and he shouted out angrily: "Go away! Have your breakfast elsewhere! Or may you be eaten by a tiger!"

Hearing this, Guno pulled away the straw and found

his companion. Koyo came out with the kris, and they resumed their journey.

They talked as they went, and they reasoned this way: The first time they found the kris they found it together. Then Koyo found it where Guno had hidden it, and afterwards Guno found it where Koyo had hidden it. Under the circumstances they each owned an equal share. So when they arrived in Tuban they sold the kris and divided the money between them.

The Learned Men

Guno and Koyo decided that they would travel together and use their wits to gain wealth and riches for themselves. Guno said: "Let us pretend to be learned men."

"Yes," Koyo said eagerly, "I have always wanted to be a learned man. I shall be Hakim Koyo, the well-known doctor from Surabaya."

"As for me," Guno said, "I shall be known as Hadji Guno, a religious scholar who has made the pilgrimage to Mecca."

And so they began their journey, talking and planning, each making suggestions as to how they would become rich. When Koyo addressed Guno, he called him Hadji, and spoke respectfully; and when Guno spoke to Koyo, he called him Hakim and said his words with great dignity. Each of them felt very profoundly the burden of his newly found position in life.

Guno quoted from the Koran, which he could not read, and Koyo explained how to cure sicknesses he had never heard of. They treated each other with the greatest honor and politeness.

As they approached a small mountain village, they saw a boy driving buffalo before him. "Which of us do you suppose he will regard as the greatest philosopher?" Guno said. "Most likely it will be me, because of his good upbringing in religious matters."

"On the contrary, he will recognize me first, for the

works of a hakim are known to Moslem and pagan alike," Koyo replied.

But when they approached, the boy said simply: "Good morning, old men."

Koyo said: "What! Is this the way one speaks to a famous hakim from Surabaya? What impudence!"

"Yes," Guno said, "what bad upbringing, to address a hadji in this manner!"

Then the boy said: "Where are you traveling, old farmers?"

"Is this the respect due to a learned man and a holy one who has made the pilgrimage?" Koyo said sternly. "How dare you speak to us so rudely?"

"I meant no harm," the boy said, "for certainly there is nothing in your appearance to distinguish you from other men."

"So!" Guno shouted. "He goes from bad to worse!"

"Yes!" Koyo added. "Not satisfied with his insult, he stretches it further!"

"How could I tell you are a doctor and a holy man?" the boy said. "You look and talk just like the people in my village."

"You ignorant buffalo boy," Koyo shouted, "don't you recognize scholars when you see them?"

And angrily Guno and Koyo seized hold of the boy and decided to take him with them as a servant. But the boy said: "Old men, I don't wish to go with you."

"If he will not walk, we must carry him," Guno said.

"Yes," Koyo echoed, "if the impudent buffalo boy does not walk, we shall carry him."

So Koyo took the boy's feet and Guno took his arms, and they began to carry him. After a while Guno said: "This end is heavier, let us change." So Koyo took the boy by the shoulders and Guno by the feet, and they carried him farther, stopping now and then to change ends. When they came to a spring, they set him down and ordered him to bring them water, but he refused. So Guno and Koyo went and brought water for the boy, who lay on the ground in the shade. When they came to a village, they ordered him to go and buy food for them, but he refused, so Koyo went and brought back food for Guno and the boy.

Carrying their servant this way, Koyo the Hakim and Guno the Hadji struggled up and down the trails. At night they were too tired to discuss learned subjects.

In the morning they slung the boy up between them and carried him on their shoulders. After a while Koyo the scholar said: "Let us stop, I have made a great scientific discovery." They stopped, and standing on the trail, Koyo continued: "Haven't you noticed how much heavier our servant is than when we first found him?"

"Yes," Guno said, "but it was a nonreligious matter, so I said nothing. There is nothing to explain it in the Koran."

"Perhaps it is his lack of exercise," Koyo said. "He should do more walking."

But the boy refused to walk or do services for the two men, so they continued to carry him and bring him food and water.

At last, one evening, exhausted by their efforts, Guno and Koyo plotted to escape from their servant. When they thought he was sleeping, they arose and started to slip quietly away, but the boy was awake, and he called to them: "Wait, old men, where are you going?"

"Is this the way one talks to a hakim?" Koyo said weakly.

"Or to a hadji?" Guno added.

They came back then and slept, and in the morning they again had to carry their servant. That night, exhausted, they again tried to slip away, but the boy stopped them. "Where are you going tonight, old men?" he asked.

"Why we were going into the great city of Jakarta to buy some food for all of us," Koyo said.

"I think you were trying to run away from me," the boy said.

"Not at all," Guno said. "I'll tell you what; *you* go into Jakarta to get the food."

"Oh no, you would run away while I am gone," the boy said.

"Will we never be rid of this unwelcome guest?" Koyo said angrily.

"Yes, why does he dog our footsteps?" Koyo echoed.

"I think we shall have to take him back where he comes from," Guno said.

"Yes, why do people always tag after scholars and philosophers?" Koyo added.

So in the morning Guno the Hadji and Koyo the Hakim hoisted the boy on their shoulders and began the long journey back to the village where they had found him.

The War of the Plants

A MALAYAN JUNGLE TALE

It is said that Gadong the jungle yam, Dagun the ground vine of the forest, and Jagong the maize plant were talking together in the men's house, telling stories and making boasts. First one bragged of his prowess, then the other.

And the jungle yam said: "Listen to this. If all the rice in the world disappeared, the people would depend most on the yam for food. It is I who would feed them all."

Hearing this, the maize plant replied: "How can this be so? If such a thing came to pass that there was no more rice, people would certainly depend most on me."

The jungle vine said: "How can you make such ridiculous assertions? If there were no more rice, no one would hear of either of you. On the lips of all people would be only my name, Dagun, and I would be sought out by all food gatherers everywhere."

They argued this way, and their boasting became hot and angry. Kachang the bean came to the men's house and listened, and he said: "How can you go on? When one speaks, the others do not listen. Who can decide this great debate except King Solomon?"

So the maize, the ground vine, and the yam went before King Solomon, saying: "Decide which of us is right, that the argument can be settled."

The maize plant said to Solomon: "Would I not be the greatest if there were no rice for men?" And the jungle yam said: "Would I not be the one to feed all mankind?"

And the ground vine said: "Do I not grow in the greatest abundance and am I not the sweetest?"

Solomon said: "All of you have your virtues, but Jagong is more nearly right; it is maize the people would seek if there were no more rice."

They went away, but the ground vine and the jungle yam were angry. Together they went looking for weapons, and they found a thorn on the thorn tree, and they took it and followed the trail of the maize plant. Jagong, the maize plant, he went seeking poison for arrows so that he could fight them. He found some and put poison on the tips of his arrows and went out to meet his enemies.

They saw each other and began to fight. The yam thrust his spear at the maize, wounding him; the cuts received in the battle can be seen today on an ear of corn. It was the jungle yam that was responsible.

The maize plant put an arrow in his bow and wounded the jungle yam; the poison from the arrow's tip, it went into the yam's body, and even today man has to remove the poison before he eats of the yam.

In the struggle, the jungle vine was pushed and pulled this way and that, and bent all out of shape. Whereas once it was tall and straight, it became twisted and crooked, as it remains to this day.

Other plants of the forest reported to King Solomon, saying: "The yam, the maize, and the vine are having a great battle."

But Solomon replied: "Let them fight until their anger has cooled."

The battle went on for twenty-one days, while all living things gathered to watch. There were trees of the forest that crowded close to watch the fight, and some of them received blows meant for the fighters. To this day their bark shows the scars of their wounds. The melons were slow to move when the fighters came their way; they were pushed this way and that, and the skin was worn off their under side which touches the ground. Therefore the skin on the under side of the melon is still pale. The bamboo was frightened by the noise. It stood far away and stretched itself as high as it could to see; for this reason the bamboo is now tall and thin. The noise and fury of the battle were altogether too great for the marsh grass; it ran off and stood at the edge of the water, where it is still found.

When twenty-one days passed, King Solomon ordered the fight to stop. And he said to the fighters: "Because you do not live well together, henceforth you will live apart, each in a separate place."

To Dagun the ground vine he said: "As for you, you will lie down, and from this time on you will crawl on your belly."

To Gadong the jungle yam he said: "From today to the end of time you will sit down in the ground."

To Jagong the maize he said: "You will henceforth stay away from the jungle, and you will stand in the open fields."

So it is, to this day. The yam must be dug from the ground where he sits. The ground vine crawls on his belly. And the maize stands stiff and straight in the clearings, where the sun beats down upon his head.

Maui the Great

It is said that in the early days man didn't have a barb for his spear or a trap door for his eel pot. It was the god Maui who invented these things. In the beginning, when the gods lived on the island of Bolotu, the other islands were at the bottom of the sea. It was Maui who brought them to the surface. In the early days man didn't know how to make fire. It was Maui who brought the knowledge of fire-making from the underworld. The sun moved across the skies so swiftly that the days were short, and Maui slowed it down so that the days were longer. The sky was pressing down against the earth, and Maui raised it up where it is to-day. It was Maui who invented the first kite, and it was Maui who imprisoned the winds. All these and many more great things Maui did.

When he was born, he was small and misshapen, and his mother abandoned him in the wilderness by the edge of the sea. But he was cared for by the sea gods, and taught wisdom by his ancestor in the sky, Tama-nui-ki-te-rangi. A time came when Maui decided to return to the earth to find his family. When he arrived, he came upon his brothers playing the game called *riti* with their spears. There was Tango-loa, and he threw his spear. There was Hemoana-uli-uli, and he threw his spear. There was Hiku-leo, and he threw his spear. They hurled their spears against a large rock to see which of them could make his spear bounce the greatest distance. Maui stood and watched them. When they saw him, they laughed because he was misshapen. He was filled with anger. He threw his spear at the rock, and it shattered the rock into many pieces. He shouted: "I am Maui, your brother!"

But they refused to believe him and called for their mother. She came and said: "You aren't my child. My children are these three."

Maui replied: "Didn't you desert me in the wilderness by the edge of the sea?"

And his mother said: "Yes, it is so. I had forgotten, thinking you were dead." She spoke in sorrow, and rejoiced then that Maui had come back.

After that Maui lived among his people. But he was not like his brothers. He played tricks on them and made them angry. But he also taught them things that he had learned from his ancestor in the sky. He designed the barb for fishing spears, so that the fish wouldn't fall off when they were pierced. He fashioned the trap door for the eel pot, so that once the eels were inside they could not find their way out.

Though Maui's brothers learned much from him, they resented him. When they went fishing in their canoes, they tried to leave him behind because they couldn't stand his tricks and jokes. When he succeeded in coming with them in the canoe, they would not give him bait, so that he couldn't interfere with their fishing. "Give me bait for my hook," he would say. And they would reply: "There is no bait for you."

But under his belt Maui carried a magic fishhook made from the jawbone of an ancient ancestor. He took it out one day and baited it with a sacred bird and cast it into the deepest water. The fish he caught was so large that he couldn't pull it in, and he asked his brothers to help him. They pulled together, and the great fish rose slowly to the top of the water. It rested there a moment, and then the fishline tautened and broke with a noise like thunder. The

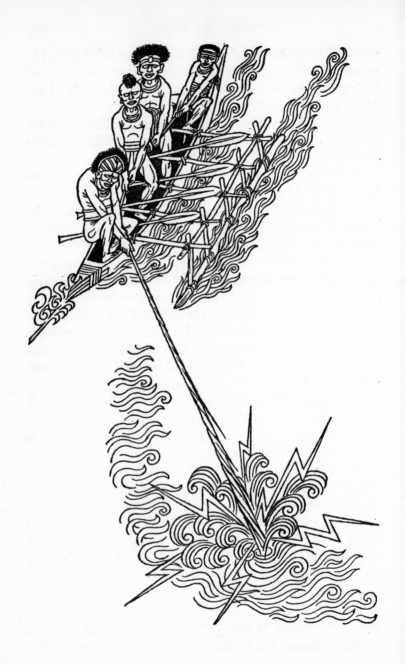

great fish, which was really land from below the sea, broke into pieces and became islands.

The brothers resolved not to take Maui fishing with them any more. One day they went to their canoe before sunrise, hoping to leave Maui behind. But Maui had heard them talking, and already he was hidden beneath the footboards in the bottom of the canoe. When they were far from shore, one of them said: "How good it is not to have Maui with us today!"

Maui threw off the boards that covered him and shouted: "Did someone call my name? I am here!" The brothers looked at the distant shore and saw that it was too far to return, so Maui stayed.

He took out his magic fishhook and said: "Give me some bait." But they refused to give him bait, so he struck his nose and made the blood run. He smeared his hook with blood and lowered it into the water.

His brothers caught no fish, and they said to him: "Why do you fish here, when there are no fish?" But he let his line out, and it went deeper and deeper into the sea until it touched the bottom. "Why are you so stubborn?" his brothers said. "There are no fish here."

Maui laughed and waited. At last there was a powerful tug on his line, and the canoe trembled. "Throw your line away," his brothers said, "or our canoe will be destroyed." But Maui held on firmly. Slowly, slowly the monster of the deep came upward. When it reached the surface, Maui's brothers cried out in awe, for it covered all the water as far as their eyes could see. Maui and his brothers leaped on the back of the monster to cut off meat while it struggled. Where they cut with their knives, there came to be ravines, and where the monster's skin became wrinkled as it thrashed around, mountains formed. Never again did the great fish sink below the water. It remained where it was and came to be known as Te-ika-a-maui, The Fish That Maui Caught. Today it is known as New Zealand.

Many days passed, and Maui and his brothers sat drinking together. Maui said: "I am weary of doing nothing. Prepare my canoe. We shall sail to distant waters to fish."

"Are there no fish here in Bolotu that we must sail to far-off seas?" said his brothers.

"Are you afraid?" Maui said.

So they prepared the canoe, and they sailed. After many days the brothers put down the sail, and Maui lowered his magic fishhook into the water. When he felt a mighty tug upon the line, he called his brothers to help him. As they hauled, the blue water grew dark. A great shadow was rising from the bottom. And from the sea there burst into view a mighty land with many mountains. They gazed upon the sight with wonder. The brothers said: "Are not the mountains too high?" And Maui replied by leaping onto the land and stamping the mountains down so that they were smaller. Thus was the island of Ata fished up from the depths of the sea.

After Ata, Maui fished up other islands. There were Tonga, Samoa, and Fiji. There were Papa-langi, Vavau, and Maabai. There were many others. All the islands of the sea, they were brought to the surface by Maui. After that, he and his brothers returned to Bolotu.

In those early days the sky pressed close to the ground, and Maui determined that the sky should be raised. He went out and saw that it was resting on the tops of the trees and the plants. He took hold with his hands and raised the sky to the mountain tops. He rested for a while, and then he pushed the sky where it is found today. The leaves of the plants and trees remain flat from having held up the sky so long before Maui moved it.

As time passed, Maui noticed that the days were too short for people to gather their food or dry their tapa cloth, for Tama-nui-a-te-ra, the sun, came up, soared across the sky, and set without any consideration for the needs of man. The god Maui resolved to make the sun slow down.

Maui's mother made magic ropes for him out of the hair of his sister Hina, and then she sent Maui to his grandmother for more help. He found his blind grandmother cooking bananas, and as she placed the bananas on the ground, Maui stole them. When she reached for them with her hand, they were gone. She said: "Who has taken the bananas?" And Maui said: "It is I, Maui, your grandson."

"Why have you taken the bananas?" she asked.

"It was only a joke," Maui answered, and then he told her why he had come.

The blind grandmother presented Maui with a magic club, and he went back to find his brothers.

"We are going to tie the sun and make him go slower so that the people have time for their work," he said.

At first his brothers refused, saying: "No, how can it be done? The sun's heat is terrible and will burn anything that comes close."

Maui said to them: "You have seen what I can do. I have raised the sky. I have raised great islands from the bottom of the sea. How can you doubt me?"

In this way Maui persuaded his brothers. They made a net out of the ropes their mother had provided, and when it was finished, they began their journey to the edge of the world where the sun came out each morning. Many months passed, and at last in the darkness of night they arrived. They placed their net over the opening through which the sun would pass, and waited.

In the morning Tama-nui-a-te-ra came through in a great rush and found himself entangled in the net. He struggled to get free, but the brothers held the net firmly and threw other ropes around the legs of the sun and tied them. Tama-nui-a-te-ra thrashed from side to side as he felt the ropes grow tighter. He took the ropes in his hands and tried to tear them apart, but they were too strong. Then Maui seized his magic war club and went forward and began to beat the sun with it. The sun fought back and threw out a mighty burst of heat, which drove the brothers back, but Maui stood his ground and fought. At last the sun cried out:

"I am the mighty Tama-nui-a-te-ra! What have I done? Why do you beat me this way?"

"Because you refuse to go slowly and give the people enough time to gather their food and dry their tapa cloth. They are hungry," Maui replied.

"I have no time to waste," Tama-nui-a-te-ra said.

So they fought again, and at last, wounded and weakened, the sun cried: "Stop! I am wounded! I will move slowly!"

Then Maui stopped fighting, and he removed the net. Tama-nui-a-te-ra went on his way, and he kept his promise, for he was wounded and could not move as fast as before. Since that day the people have had time to gather their food and dry their tapa cloth. But some of the ropes that Maui and his brothers put on the sun are still there; they can be seen sometimes as long bright beams of light piercing through the clouds.

There were still other things that Maui did. In those early days man didn't have the secret of how to make fire. Maui determined to get the secret, so he went down into the underworld to see Mafuike, the guardian of fire. He asked her for an ember to take back with him. She gave him one of her burning fingernails. When he came to a river, he stopped and thought: "This is fire, but this is not the secret of how to make it." So he threw the flame into the river and returned to Mafuike, asking for another ember. She gave him another burning fingernail, and when he came to the river, he threw that one in the water also. He went back again and again, and each time she gave him another flaming fingernail. When he appeared for the tenth time, Mafuike was enraged. She chased him out of the underworld in great fury. But Maui was so fast that she couldn't catch him. He taunted her as he ran, and finally in violent anger she took her tenth flaming fingernail and hurled it at him.

It fell in the grass and set the fields and forests on fire. Maui fled before the onrushing flames, which threatened to destroy everything. In great distress, Maui called on the rain for help. The rain fell and halted the spreading fire. Seeing that the world's last fire was being extinguished, Mafuike the fire deity picked up bits of fire from the ground and hid them in the trees.

Since that day fire has remained in the world, hidden in the trees where Mafuike put it. But man knows now how to bring it out of hiding, by rubbing one kind of wood on another.

The Great Lizard of Nimple

FROM THE ISLAND OF YAP

People sometimes talk of Yap as a single island, but it is really four. There is Tamil; there is Map; there is Nimigil, the largest; and the smallest, it is Rumung. But in ancient times they were one, and there was no water separating them. It was Galuf the giant sea lizard that broke Yap into four pieces. His hiding place was in the harbor of Nimple, and from this place he preyed upon all living things. Men were afraid to sail their canoes across the water of the harbor, because Galuf would catch them and eat them. He was swift as the swiftest boat, and once he had begun to pursue a victim, there was no escaping from him.

In the village of Atiliu there was a canoe builder by the name of Pirow. Often he listened to tales of the giant sea lizard. Often he stood with his friends at the water's edge waiting for canoes that never returned.

One day Pirow said to his wife: "I shall destroy this monster of the sea." He took his ax and went out among the big trees. He searched until he found a tall straight tree called biyuuch, and he cut it down. He took his knives and adze and began to fashion a canoe. Many days he worked. The canoe was finished. He carried it down to the water. There he built an outrigger for the canoe and made a sail.

Then he went fishing and caught a fish and brought it to his wife. He said: "Smoke this fish for me. I will see if I can sail my new canoe around the island before you have

140

finished." He entered his canoe and sailed around the island of Yap. When he returned, his wife gave him the smoked fish. It was done. He said: "The canoe is too slow."

When morning came, he went again among the big trees and found a tree called lach. He cut it down with his ax and began to make another canoe. Every day he worked. In many days the canoe was finished. Again he gave his wife a fish to smoke, and again he sailed his craft around the island. He returned and found that the fish was smoked. He said: "This canoe is swifter than the first, but it is not swift enough."

Four more canoes were built by Pirow, each a little swifter than the one before, but none was fast enough to suit him. So he went once more among the big trees and fashioned another canoe out of the tree called thow, which gives breadfruit. Once more he gave his wife a fish to smoke for him. He sailed around the island of Yap, and this time, when he returned, he saw that his wife was still sitting before the fire with the fish. Pirow said: "This canoe is the fastest of all."

That night the canoe builder did not sleep in his own house with his wife. He slept in the all-men's-house. In the morning he took his fishing raft and went to the lagoon. He descended below the water, looking for a giant clam. All morning he was in the water. At last, deep among the coral, he found what he was looking for. The giant clam was so large that Pirow had to struggle to bring it to his raft. He took it then to his canoe and lashed the giant clam to his outrigger. He sailed the canoe to the harbor of Nimple. There he heard the voice of the great lizard calling to him.

The canoe made of the wood of the thow tree sped over the water, and Galuf the great lizard pursued it. The lizard saw at last that he could not catch Pirow, and he called out: "Be kind, wait for me, I am tired."

The canoe builder laughed, saying: "You want to eat me."

"I will not eat you," the great lizard said. "Forgive me for the bad intentions I had a while ago."

"Very well," Pirow said, "come into the canoe."

"How shall I come, by the prow or the stern?" the lizard asked.

"Come by way of the outrigger," Pirow said. "That will be easier."

The lizard was glad. He wanted to destroy the outrigger and capsize the canoe. Then he would seize Pirow. Galuf came close and threw himself upon the outrigger

with force. He fell into the mouth of the giant clam. The shells closed upon Galuf's head. The lizard thrashed his tail violently back and forth. By accident the tail lashed the northern part of Yap, cutting away a piece of land, the island that is now called Rumung. Again his tail lashed against the land, cutting away Map. The third and last time his tail struck the land, it severed Tamil from Nimigil. Then Galuf died.

Thus Yap was cut into four parts. Thus it has remained.

When Pirow returned with the news that the great sea lizard was dead, there was feasting. Since then men have been able to sail safely across the water of Nimple Harbor.

Notes on the Stories

The Scholar of Kosei (Korea)

Based on an oral version of an old Korean story, this tale features a kind of humor that is much loved in all parts of the world—the scholar so immersed in his profound thoughts that he loses touch with reality. In eastern Europe the same theme appears in a cycle of tales about the people of Helm, a town in Poland; in this latter version the scholar places his shoes on the ground pointing to his destination, but a prankster turns them around so that they point toward the place from which the traveler has come.

The Tiger's Whisker (Korea)

Recorded from an oral narration by a Korean seaman, Lee Bok. The hermit sage in this story believes that experience is the best teacher. As in many folk tales, the conclusion is preceded by a "test," but in this case the test is laden with considerable meaning.

The Tiger's Minister of State (Burma)

In Burma, as elsewhere in Southeast Asia, the rabbit or hare is a shrewd and clever character whose adventures and exploits are comparable to those of Brer Rabbit in the United States, the spider trickster in West Africa, and the mouse deer of Indonesia and Malaya. This particular tale has an especially ironic point to make—that a politician, to be successful, must be blind to certain acts of his superiors.

The Trial of the Stone (Burma)

A story from the Shan area of eastern Burma. The Shan people are an ethnic group of Southeast Asia, found in Thailand and China. This is a comedy situation in which the village magistrate achieves a measure of justice, or at least relief, for the boy by a silly ruse.

The Hidden Treasure of Khin (Burma)

A tale of traditional Asian character, in which the father bequeaths a riddle to his son that results in contentment and prosperity.

The King Who Ate Chaff (Burma)

Based on a story collected by Maung Htin Aung, and published in *Burmese Folk Tales*, Bombay, 1948. Used with the kind permission of Oxford University Press. There is a Japanese tale about a bell that was taken from a certain monastery and installed in a new place; whenever people tried to ring the bell, however, it said, "Take me back."

The Musician of Tagaung (Burma)

This story, heard from a Burmese informant, comments upon the vanity of success and notes that a "reputation" may be built out of thin air. The development of a family hero and genius out of some old dusty harps recalls the Ethiopian tale, "The Hero of Adi Nifas," in which a hero is conjured up out of the fact that a man seems to have disappeared. In this latter story a group of travelers, thinking that one of their party is missing, spontaneously attribute to the supposedly missing man a great single-handed combat with a leopard. (See *The Fire on the Mountain* by Harold Courlander and Wolf Leslau.)

The Rice Puller of Chaohwa (China)

Based on a translation by Hsin-Chih Lee and Cho-Feng L. Lee of a story recorded by Mencius (Meng-tse), who lived during the third and second centuries B.C.

The Spear and Shield of Huan-Tan (China)

An ancient tale, translated by Hsin-Chih Lee and Cho-Feng L. Lee from the book *Han-Fei-tzu.*

The Ambassador from Chi (China)

Translated by Hsin-Chih Lee and Cho-Feng L. Lee from the ancient book *Yen-tzu Chun Chiu.*

The King of the Forest (China)

Based on a tale translated by Hsin-Chih Lee and Cho-Feng L. Lee from the ancient book *Chan-kuo-Cher.*

The Trial at Avichára-pura (Ceylon)

Rewritten from a tale in "Sinhalese Folk-Lore Stories" by W. Knight James, in the *Journal of the Ceylon Branch of the Royal Asiatic Society,* 1882. According to the original collector, *vichára* signifies "inquiry" and *pura* means "city." Thus Avichára-pura is "the city of the inquiry (or trial)." A very similar Middle Eastern form of the story is told in Egypt and appears under the title "The Judgement of Karakoush" in *Arabian Romances and Folk Tales* by Habib T. Katibah, New York, 1929. In the Egyptian version, too, the story is associated with a saying: "Like the judgement of Karakoush."

The Prince of the Six Weapons (India)

One of the intriguing elements of this *Jataka* tale is the combat between the young man and the monster, in which the prince's right hand, left hand, right foot, left foot, and head become entangled and helpless. This sequence, as well as the situation, has been preserved exactly in the West African tale of Anansi and the gum man and the Brer Rabbit tale involving the tar baby. Variants of the theme of getting stuck to the monster are known throughout the world, though usually it is a fashioned figure that traps the victim. Retold from the version in *Indian Fairy Tales,* by Joseph Jacobs, London, 1892.

The Man from Kailasa (India)

Taken from "The Good Wife and the Bad Husband" in *Folk-lore in Southern India*, by Pandit S. M. Natesa Sastri, Bombay, 1884. This is a south Indian variant of a tale fairly widespread in southern and southeastern Asia. An Indonesian version of the story is to be found in Courlander, *Kantchil's Lime Pit*, New York, 1950.

Krishna the Cowherd (India)

This story of the god Krishna has been extracted from the *Harivamsha*, a supplementary book to the *Mahabharata*, and is only a fragmentary part of the long epic. It is presented here in greatly simplified form, divested of most of the mystical complexities of the original. No mention is made, for example, that Krishna is the eighth avatar of the god Vishnu and a reincarnation of the god Narayana, nor is reference made to the mystical aspects of Krishna's birth. In the Hindu mythology Krishna's companion Balarama is a sort of mirrored reflection and another aspect of Krishna himself. It is believed by some scholars that Krishna was originally a local hero who was deified after death and eventually became absorbed into the great Hindu myth.

The Scholars and the Lion (India)

Rewritten from the translation by Arthur W. Ryder of the *Panchatantra*. Used with the kind permission of the copyright holder, Winifred M. Ryder, and the University of Chicago Press. The central incident of this ancient tale has been preserved in contemporary folklore. The putting together of a dead creature's bones, putting on flesh, sinews, and so forth, occurs, among other places, in West African lore. In one such tale it is the father of a family, killed in the hunt, whose bones are put together. (See *The Cow-Tail Switch*, by Harold Courlander and George Herzog, New York, 1947.) The particular import and consequence of the act in this ancient Indian tale are unusual. In many widespread tales, however, an animal saved by man (or another animal) turns on him and attempts to eat him.

The Traveler and the Nut Tree (Kashmir)

Originally collected by J. Hinton Knowles and published in *Folk-Tales of Kashmir*, London, 1893.

The Debt (Kashmir)

Based on a tale in the Knowles collection, *ibid*. The story recalls the Biblical tale of Solomon judging between two women who claim the same baby.

The Boy and the Cloth (Kashmir)

This tale of the slow-witted boy is a compound of fragments recorded by Knowles, *ibid*.

The Wrestler of Kyushu (Japan)

Taken from a Japanese informant. The picture of a great wrestler standing without giving quarter to a monstrous snake would appear to have special meaning to Japanese aware of the traditions of Sumo wrestling. Men who participated in this sport were large, heavy, and often of great strength, unlike those who went in for Judo, better known in the West.

The Counting of the Crocodiles (Japan)

This version of "The Bridge of Crocodiles" (it is also one of the Kantchil cycle of tales of Indonesia) is presented as a complete story, as I originally heard it. In some collections of Japanese lore, however, it is presented as a part of a longer, picaresque story in which good and bad human beings are involved. It is my belief that this combination of the bridge of crocodiles theme with other materials doesn't show off the hare's adventure to best advantage. For the Indonesian variant, different only in language and in the fact that the hero (Kantchil, the mouse deer) doesn't lose his tail, see Courlander, *Kantchil's Lime Pit*, New York, 1950.

Abunuwas the Trickster (Arabia)

Abunuwas is a favorite trickster throughout the Islamic world. The original Abu Nuwas, or Nawas, was a poet in the court of Harun-al-Rashid. He was noted for his many escapades, and through the years a vast number of apocryphal tales have become attached to his name. A Somali tale about Abunuwas is to be found in Courlander and Leslau, *The Fire on the Mountain*, New York, 1950. Some episodes in the story told here were taken from *Abu Nuwas in Life and Legend*, by W. H. Ingrams, privately printed at Port Luis, Mauritius, 1933; all of them are known in Arabia, however, as well as in other Arab and Arabic-speaking lands. Permission for use of some portions of this tale was given by the United Nations Women's Guild and Whittlesey House, those portions having appeared in *Ride with the Sun*, edited by Harold Courlander, New York, 1955.

The Spotted Rug (Arabia)

Taken from an oral narration. Variants of the story are known in Eastern Europe.

The Philosophers of King Darius (Persia)

This story is a fusion of two variants, one oral, the other written. The oral version was given by an Arabian informant, while the written version appears in the *Books of Esdras*, a part of the Biblical Apocrypha that developed among the Jews of Alexandria. The oral rendition had simply an anonymous ruler, while the *Esdras* names Darius the King of the Persians. In the *Books of Esdras*, couched in remarkable and poetic language, the things advocated as the strongest in life were wine, the king, woman, and finally truth. The oral version omitted wine (probably because of the Islamic strictures against alcohol), but in addition to the other items it included man and wealth. The tale as given here includes all of the arguments of both versions. In the *Esdras* the contest is won by a Jew named Zorobel, and as a prize Darius agrees to commission the rebuilding of the destroyed temple in Jerusalem.

The assignment of this tale to Persian tradition is merely a convenience, dictated only by the fact that Darius figures in it. In modern form it may not be known in Persia (Iran). In its literary form one would have to acknowledge its Oriental-Jewish source.

Dinner for the Monk (Laos)

Based on a story in *Laos Folk-Lore of Farther India*, by Katherine Fleeson, New York, 1899. The monk being tugged between two dinners—ending in nothing to eat—recalls an adventure in which the West African spider, Anansi, is pulled between two feasts by ropes. (See "Two Dinners for Anansi" in Courlander, *The Hat-Shaking Dance*, New York, 1957.)

The Well Diggers (Indonesia)

The two foolish characters of this tale, Guno and Koyo, are a well-known low comedy team in Indonesian lore. Guno means "helpful" and Koyo means "rich"; neither of the characters ever lives up to his name. Another tale in this cycle appears in *Kantchil's Lime Pit, ibid.*

Guno and Koyo and the Kris (Indonesia)

Another episode in the adventures of Guno and Koyo. A similar tale is told in Ceylon.

The Learned Men (Indonesia)

Still another ludicrous performance of Guno and Koyo (see above).

The War of the Plants (Malaya)

Based on an oral variant and a tale in *Fables and Folktales from an Eastern Forest* by W. Skeat, Cambridge, 1901. A tale accounting for the characteristics of various plants. In the setting of this tale there are no animals. Vegetable tales of this kind are not often encountered, animals being more suitable protagonists. But vegetable tales do exist in many traditions. A somewhat similar battle between vegetables takes place in a tale told by the Ashanti people of Ghana, West Africa.

Maui the Great (Polynesia)

Maui is one of the great Polynesian culture heroes. Different tales are told about him in different islands, and some elements of Polynesian lore are found also in Melanesia. Some of the incidents depicted here are from the Maori of New Zealand, some from Hawaii, Tonga, and other Pacific islands. In certain Polynesian islands the feats of Maui are attributed, in part, to another demigod, Tane. An interesting aspect of the Maui legend is the coincidence of the trickster and the culture hero. Maui is both an unscrupulous jokester and a benefactor of the human race. Even the most serious business is interlarded with his pranks. When he goes to his grandmother for a magic war club, for example, he makes his presence known by stealing her bananas. This combination of trickster and creator or benefactor runs through much of the world's folklore and legend, including American Indian and West African. In Ghana the spider trickster is credited with deeds accounting for the beginning of certain things, such as the moon. It is interesting to recall that in the Krishna epic in this collection, the hero of that myth was noted in his infancy and youth for his pranks. Some portions of this tale as given here appeared previously in *Ride with the Sun* (*ibid*), and are included with the kind permission of the United Nations Women's Guild and Whittlesey House.

The Great Lizard of Nimple (Yap Island)

Many of the tales of Micronesia, like those of other Pacific islands, account for the beginning of natural phenomena, particularly the formation of the islands themselves (see "Maui the Great"). This story was narrated by John Mangefel of the island of Yap, from his own memory.